PRINCESS

By

Courtney Cole

Book One

The American Princess series

ISBN: 0615602940
ISBN-13: 978-0615602943

DEDICATION

To my husband.
Everything about you makes me smile.
Thank you for always asking,
"When do I get to see you?"

"Being a princess isn't all it's cracked up
to be."
--Diana, Princess of Wales

Chapter One

"You want me to wear *what?*"

Sydney's slender fingers, which were lightly twirling her dark blonde hair, abruptly stopped moving as her mouth gaped open.

Late afternoon sunlight poured in through the floor-to-ceiling windows, illuminating her delicate features and shining into her eyes, but she ignored it. She was focused on the outrageous request that she had just heard from her boyfriend's lips.

On the other end of the cell phone, Christian repeated himself even though he knew perfectly well that Sydney had heard him the first time. His voice was as velvety-smooth and assured as ever, a perfect reflection of the confidence behind it. It had never entered his mind that Sydney might say no because she never had.

"I want you to come over wearing only your coat.   Come completely naked underneath."

Sydney snapped her mouth closed and then closed her eyes for good measure, too.

"You've got to be kidding. My mother is home…" Her voice trailed off uncertainly as she twisted a sapphire ring round and round on her middle finger.

"Do I detect a note of fear in your voice, Syd? I know that can't be right. The Sydney Ross that I know and love isn't afraid of anything."

She was completely aware that Christian was goading her because he knew that more than anything, she hated to be thought of as scared. She hated it even more than a week long juice fast. She had never turned down a dare and she was slightly annoyed that Christian was exploiting that weakness.   That said, she still couldn't ignore it. It wasn't in her nature.

"I'm not afraid," she insisted. "But May isn't exactly long coat weather. Someone's going to notice. Why don't you come over here wearing only your football pads? That would be more entertaining...at least for me."

She smiled and let herself relax, sinking into the softness of her damask chaise lounge. Laughing things off almost always worked when she didn't want to do something. It wasn't effective today, however. Christian was stubbornly persistent.

"Syd, I miss you. I haven't seen you in days. Your mom is home. Mine's not. I just want some alone time. After we leave for college, we're not going to be able to see each other much. And that's only a few months away. It's rainy out so just wear a rain coat."

And that was it. Her heart melted into a pool around her toes. Christian was charming even when he begged. How could she say no? She couldn't fault him for wanting to spend time with her. He was right. Pretty soon they would be going to separate colleges. And it always got her when Christian, the strong self-assured guy that he was, got sentimental and told her how much he needed her.

"I want to see you, too," she murmured softly, relenting. "I'll be there in twenty."

Tossing down her phone, she gazed around her bedroom. Designer clothing was draped over every piece of furniture, but she wasn't concerned by the mess. Their housekeeper, Stella, was deep-cleaning today and would hit her room at some point. And it wasn't as though she needed to find something to wear. Instead, she began taking her clothing off, laying each item piece-by-piece on the plush white sofa in her sitting area until she stood naked in the center of the room.

She knew she didn't have anything to be embarrassed of. Long, lean legs. Flat tummy. Golden-hued skin. Warm brownish-hazel eyes, honey blonde hair, a light smattering of freckles on the nose that she had inherited from her mother. She gave a long sigh. She would do. Although she did wish that her boobs were bigger. A healthy C cup instead of the small B that she currently sported would be nice.

With another sigh of resignation, she continued her nude jaunt into her walk-in closet to sift through the winter section. Her closet was the size of a normal person's entire bedroom, crammed full with racks of expensive clothing and stacks of shoes, so finding the longest feasible coat took a few minutes. She needed to find one that wouldn't stand out in May. Obviously, she couldn't wear an ankle-length parka even though she wanted to.

She finally selected a mid-thigh length Burberry plaid rain coat, pulling it out and holding it up against her to judge its length. It was appropriate for the weather and was long enough to cover her naked butt. Barely.

Good Lord. She couldn't believe she was going to do this. But hell would have to freeze over before she backed down. She cinched the belt at her narrow waist and didn't even glance behind her at the mirror again as she stuck her feet into a pair of heels, grabbed her purse and left the room.

As she descended the winding grand staircase, there wasn't a sound other than the low hum of the vacuum from a distant location in the house. She knew it was Stella. Her mother would rather die than do housework.

Nearing the bottom step, Sydney felt a brief moment of dizziness and chided herself silently. There was no reason to get worked up. She could totally do this. She paused to take a deep breath and the dizzy spell passed.

"Mom?" she called as she reached the bottom stair and stepped down onto the wide marble floor of the foyer. Her heels clacked loudly as she walked across the glossy stone.

"Mom?"

No answer. Maybe she would luck out and her mother wouldn't be home. Then she could just leave a note and her mother wouldn't examine her appearance with the hawk-like eyes that missed nothing.

Wearing only a coat was not the behavior of a senator's daughter. Just as the thought crossed her mind, a draft suddenly blew up her coat and she shivered as the cool air brushed her naked flesh. She felt infinitely naughty. She had to admit, though, she liked the feeling. It definitely spiced up her day.

The smell of freshly baked cookies led her to the kitchen. She entered just in time to find their black haired cook, Ben, pulling a tray of white chocolate macadamia cookies from the oven. His dark hair in combination with his ice blue eyes made most people do a double-take when they saw him for the first time.

"Miss Ross, you're just in time. Better get one while they're hot!"

Ben beamed his ever-present cheerful grin and motioned to a rack of her favorite cookies cooling on the massive granite expanse of counter space.

She smiled back at him and grabbed one as she walked by, burning her finger tips and once again feeling a brief wave of nausea and dizziness. She shook her head in annoyance. Sydney Ross didn't get scared. She was being silly.

"Thanks, Ben!" she called over her shoulder as she continued on through the library. She could hear him humming as she walked away and smiled to herself. She had never met someone so perpetually happy.

As she passed the sparkling glass wall of windows that framed their courtyard, she spotted her mother lounging on the stone-tiled veranda, holding an iced lemon tea in her hand and laughing wildly at something her new tennis instructor had apparently said. Sydney nibbled on her cookie as she observed them for a minute.

The guy couldn't be more than twenty years old and was hanging over Jillian Ross' shoulder, murmuring softly into her ear and rubbing her arms as he spoke.

Sydney rolled her eyes in disgust. Pathetic. As intimate as they appeared, her mother might as well sit in the guy's lap. Why her dad put up with that kind of behavior, Sydney didn't know. But then, in order for it to upset him, he would have to be home long enough to witness it. And he never was.

The scene in front of her made her sick to her stomach, making it impossible to continue watching them if she wanted to keep the cookie that she had just eaten down in her stomach where it belonged. She pulled open the heavy glass doors and stuck her head out.

"Mom? I'm going over to Christian's. I'll be back later."

Her mother barely spared her a glance.

"That's fine, Sydney. Let Ben know you won't be here for dinner."

And that was it. Jillian flipped her blonde hair over her shoulder and returned her attention to the fawning boy. He was a new one. Sydney didn't even know his name. What she did know was that his white shorts were indecently short and tight. She could easily see the bulgy outline of his man-junk.

And he was so, so obviously flirting with her mother. But then again, her mother was eating it up so it was working out nicely for him. Sydney shook her head. She shouldn't have worried that her mother would notice her lack of clothing.

If she was honest, she would have to admit that Jillian rarely noticed her at all, except for times that she thought Sydney was doing something unseemly for a girl in her position.

During those incidents, Jillian focused in on her with razor-sharp precision and an even sharper tongue. Most of their mother-daughter interactions were focused on ensuring that Sydney dressed correctly, spoke correctly and behaved correctly at every minute of any given day. It was exhausting.

At just that thought, Sydney heard her name. Her gaze snapped up and she found her mother staring at her, gesturing for her to return to the patio.

Sighing, Sydney re-opened the glass door and stood in the doorway. She could feel the tennis instructor's eyes on her body, but she ignored it.

"Yes?" she asked her mother.

"Are you eating a cookie?" Jillian's voice was frosty. Sydney fought the urge to roll her eyes. She had a cookie in her hand. Clearly, she was eating it.

"Yes," she answered simply.

"Do you realize how much sugar is in that cookie?" Jillian demanded, her pale blue eyes snapping. "It will go straight to your thighs. We don't need this right now, Sydney. Go throw it away."

The tennis instructor nodded, as though he agreed with Jillian. As though it were normal for a mother to be so agitated over a simple cookie.

"Fine," Sydney answered wearily. "I'll throw it away on my way out." She began to close the door.

"Wait," Jillian said suddenly. "Bring it here."

Sydney paused. Seriously? This was ridiculous.

But she obligingly carried the half-eaten cookie to her mother and placed it in Jillian's waiting hand. Jillian tossed it onto the stone patio and ground her heel into it.

Jillian studied her daughter's calm face. "Please remember not to eat such junk, Sydney. You're not going to be seventeen forever. You need to watch your figure. You know the public watches us. We live in a fishbowl."

Sydney nodded and closed the door silently with a click. She felt pretty sure that the public didn't care what size her thighs were, but there was no reasoning with Jillian Ross. Her mother was ridiculous, but it was usually best to simply humor her and go on with life. Sydney shook her head and continued through the house.

Stepping into the garage, she stared down the line of gleaming cars. Her father's black Cadillac was gone which meant that he was at the office. No surprise there. He practically lived in his downtown Chicago high-rise. She walked past his empty slot and her mother's white Jag to stand next to her own car- a shiny silver graduation gift. She had gotten the little Mercedes convertible two weeks ago and she had finally mastered the manual transmission, making her feel like an automotive queen.

Today she felt like a *liberated* automotive queen as she drove into their exclusive Highland Park neighborhood and idled at red lights knowing full well that she was naked under her coat. It was surprisingly exhilarating and she slipped off her shoes so that she could drive barefoot.

Enjoying the feel of her naked legs resting against the butter-soft leather of her seat, she smiled broadly at the guy in the next car, before gunning her engine when the light turned green. She smoothly cut him off so that she could make her exit.

As a result of her trademark aggressive driving, it only took her twenty minutes today to weave through Highland Park, just as she had promised. The sleek little car wound through the traffic effortlessly, purring like a jungle cat. Lucky for her, Christian lived in the same neighborhood. Downtown Chicago traffic was perpetually congested and would have taken much longer.

Christian opened the front doors just as she pulled into his drive and stood waiting for her on the top step. Sydney studied his handsome features as she got out and walked toward him, her heart thudding lightly with anticipation. As her pulse quickened, she fervently hoped that she seemed calm and cool, but she doubted that was the case.

She had a secret.

Deep down, no matter how perfect her manicure and highlights were or how well she filled out an outfit, she always felt a little insufficient. She could look in the mirror and see that she was pretty and many might even say beautiful. But it was as though she couldn't quite get her heart to understand that she was good enough. She didn't know why and she would never be able to explain it to anyone, so she didn't try. She could just hear the "poor little rich girl" jokes that would result in that kind of conversation.

Christian, on the other hand, certainly didn't suffer from inadequacy issues. With his black slacks and slate gray v-neck, he was impeccably sleek and sophisticated today which was usually the case. And he was always unflustered.

He was outrageously handsome and outlandishly cocky, two things that she loved about him. His dark hair was carefully tousled just-so and the smile he wore was perfect, the result of thousands of dollars of cosmetic dentistry. His dark blue eyes were frozen on her, as if drawing her to him. When she got close enough, he reached for her, grabbing the end of the belt to her coat.

"Chris, not on the porch!" she giggled and slapped his hand away.

Undeterred, he laughed carelessly and scooped her up in his strong arms, ignoring her half-hearted protests. As the half-back on their football team, he spent quite a lot of time working out. The results were apparent. He was built like a lean brick house and would be playing ball for Princeton next year as a Legacy student.

As he effortlessly carried her up the grand staircase to his room, he purposely moved one of his hands farther up on her leg and then farther still. She knew he was checking for clothing. She laughed and clutched his back, knowing what was to come as his hand kept moving. Her heart thudded loudly again and she closed her eyes as Christian kicked the bedroom door closed behind them.

They didn't emerge for two hours, only coming out for food. Bursting out of the bedroom when the doorbell rang, they laughed and shoved each other playfully, racing each other to get to the pizza first. They had used an abundance of calories and Sydney's stomach was growling.

Christian beat her, of course. He made it down the long stairway in three seconds flat. He threw the front door open, paid for the pizza and they collapsed on the floor in the foyer with the pizza box without bothering to get plates from the kitchen.

Sydney grinned over a slice of pizza, catching the dripping cheese with her tongue.

"You're right. We could never do this at my house. My mom would have a stroke."

Holding a finger up in the air, she appeared to get into character for a performance. Christian watched in amusement as she stuck her nose into the air, pushed her eyebrows into her hairline and mimicked her mother's haughty voice.

"Sydney, it is not appropriate for Randall Ross' daughter to eat pizza on the floor, be it marble or otherwise."

Sydney rolled her eyes as she returned to her pizza, sucking the hot cheese into her mouth. If she had a dollar for every time she was referred to as "Randall Ross' daughter," she would be a millionaire in her own right.

Christian laughed.

"We couldn't have done a lot of things at your house today, Syd. This is only the least of it. But since *my* parents are out of town..."

His voice trailed off huskily as he reached over and slid his hand up the shirt she was wearing. It was his and hung on her like a baggy knee-length dress, giving him ample room to maneuver underneath it.

She pushed his hand away.

"Again? I think not. I have to replenish my energy. Just because you're tireless, doesn't mean everyone in this room is."

She batted her eyes playfully at him as she inhaled her second slice of pizza, enjoying the forbidden grease and cheese combination. The carb count alone would be enough to give her mother a heart attack. But Sydney couldn't help but love it. No one in their right mind could ever say that Chicago had bad pizza.

"You know," Christian said thoughtfully as he watched her eat, "I think you're the first girl I've ever dated that actually eats in front of me. And you eat a lot. I don't know how you stay so skinny!" He leaned toward her. "Except for here. And here." He brushed against her curves with his hand.

"Christian! Is that all you ever think about?" she demanded in mock exasperation, knocking his fingers away.

He only laughed. They both knew full well that she was far from aggravated; that it was just a matter of time before her appetite was sated and she responded to him again.

"Why, yes. Yes, it is. But at least I'm honest." Christian's face was impish as his cobalt eyes twinkled at her. Those were eyes that a girl could get lost in. Sydney sighed.

"Yes, at least you're honest. Now calm yourself down and let me eat! Take a cold shower or something."

They were both laughing until a third, unexpected voice startled them both.

"Mr. Price?!"

The housekeeper was frozen in the arched doorway with a look of utter shock on her creased face. Sydney couldn't help but giggle. And then she was promptly embarrassed as she remembered that she was only wearing Christian's shirt. She immediately looked down to make sure that her rump was covered, tugging on the hem a little bit just to be on the safe side. This was one situation in which her long legs were not a blessing.

"Hi, Fran. Miss Ross here couldn't wait to get to the table, so we decided to eat right here. She's got a very voracious appetite."

He waggled his eyebrows at his double entendre and Sydney's cheeks burned. Christian's naughty humor was apparent and Sydney just hoped that Fran hadn't caught the double meaning.

"Don't stare, Fran. You don't want to make Sydney uncomfortable. Her father is our senator, after all."

He winked at the maid, who was still staring at them in cliché-like astonishment. Her mouth was even hanging open a little bit. Sydney hid another giggle. She couldn't help it. She laughed when she was nervous. It had gotten her into trouble more than a few times in her life.

"And I don't think my father needs to hear about this, don't you agree? In fact, why don't you take the rest of the evening off? You deserve it. You work too hard. And have I mentioned that you look beautiful today?"

Christian winked again and Fran shook her head, finally smiling at him, even though having a half-dressed girl in the house was clearly against the rules. Even if the girl was Sydney Ross. Actually, probably especially then. His parents wouldn't want him involved in any kind of political scandal.

"Mr. Price, your shenanigans are going to get me fired yet!"

The disgruntled housekeeper turned on her heel and left the room, her gray curls still shaking as she muttered under her breath but she left them alone. Christian turned to Sydney with a perfectly straight face.

"Is shenanigans a word?" he asked her and then grinned.

Sydney shook her head, even though she couldn't help but smile at the same time. Christian's humor was infectious.

"You know, this does put her in a tough spot. You really could get her fired one of these days and I'm sure she needs her job. I should go." She started to get up.

He grabbed her arm. "No, don't. You know she's been with us forever. My parents would never fire her and she won't bother us again tonight. Please? Stay a while longer?"

His eyes were beseeching and Sydney felt herself relent. Once again. She couldn't seem to help herself. She wasn't good at telling him no. She let herself sink back onto the floor.

"How do you know that she won't bother us again tonight? How many other girls have you had here like this?"

Sydney was only half-joking. Christian definitely had a reputation for being a playboy. That was something she had been quite aware of when she started dating him. For some reason, it had been part of the allure... to see if she could get him and keep him. It hadn't taken her long, which surprised her. And they had been together for five months now, a record for both of them.

"What?" His voice was full of exaggerated innocence. "Me? You've got to be kidding. Sydney, you're my first."

The over-emphasized expression of outrage on his face cracked her up and she reached over to trail her fingers through his dark hair, which he interpreted as an open invitation and moved closer to her. She promptly shrugged out of his reach.

"Um, right. Seriously. How many other girls has Fran seen you with?"

"Well, that's a difficult question, really. She's getting older and her eyesight is getting bad."

He stopped talking as he pushed her over and gently pinned her down, nuzzling the side of her neck.

"Besides, that doesn't matter anymore. I'm with you now. And you smell really good...what is that? Chanel no. 5?" He stopped talking as he kissed further down on her neck.

"Close. It's Chanel Mademoiselle and it matters to me, Christian. You were my first.

Girls always remember that. It's special. I want you to remember me, too. I don't want to be just another girl that Fran walked in on." She sighed as he nuzzled even further down on her neck toward her breasts. "I can't focus if you keep doing that."

He chuckled and mumbled, "That's sort of the point, Syd."

She closed her eyes as his hands slid over her hips. She'd worry about it later. The stone tiles of the foyer were rough against her back, but she was oblivious to it. All she concentrated on was the warm, delicious weight of Christian's body as he moved against her.

* * *

Sunshine flooded her bedroom, filling every possible crevice with light, just like it did every other afternoon. It was cheerful, optimistic and really, really bright.

Sydney squinted as sat up in her bed and then promptly clutched her stomach. It rolled harshly as her mother continued opening the blinds. She was sure that if she looked into a mirror, her skin would appear gray. In fact, she felt like the epitome of the word 'ashen,' as nausea and dizziness overwhelmed her and she groaned.

"Sydney? You cannot lie around in bed all day. We've got a photo-shoot for your father's new campaign mailing in an hour. You've got to move." Jillian's eyes did a quick once-over of her daughter and she paused mid-step. "Are you ill? You've got dark circles."

It was clear that she was more appalled than concerned. If Sydney was sick, she wouldn't photograph well. As always, they needed to portray the perfect all-American family for the photos.

"I don't feel well at all," Sydney moaned as she fell back against her pillows. "I noticed this stupid bug when I was at Christian's a couple of weeks ago. At first, I thought I just ate too much or the pizza sauce was bad or something but that can't be it because it just won't go away. I've had it too long. And I'm tired constantly. Maybe I have something like mono. Is that possible?" She looked at her mother questioningly. "I should probably go to the doctor."

"Oh, that would be just perfect, Sydney. Then I would have to explain to the world how you got Kissing Disease." Her mother was curt and unsympathetic as she stalked into Sydney's closet to yank clothes off the rack for her daughter to wear.

"Pull yourself together. You need to shower. You look like death." She tossed a cream colored v-neck sweater and a pair of linen slacks on the food of the bed.

"Ugh. I feel like death, too." Sydney groaned as she stared up at the ceiling.

She swallowed hard to battle the waves of nausea that threatened to overtake her. It didn't help. Saliva was pooling in her mouth and her breath smelled sour. The room started spinning around her and she suddenly couldn't contain it.

She lunged out of bed and barely made it to the bathroom before she started heaving. When she was finished, she curled up into a ball and rested her cheek on the cool marble floor.

"Mom?" She croaked hoarsely. "I don't think I can do the photo shoot today. I feel awful."

Jillian loomed in the bathroom door for a moment before tentatively approaching Sydney. She quickly laid the back of her elegant hand on Sydney's forehead.

"No fever. Do you have a sore throat?" As she asked, she backed quickly away, as though Sydney might have the plague.

"No. I just feel like I'm going to die any minute. I'm so nauseous!"

Her mother suddenly froze mid-step as a thought occurred to her.

"Sydney, last month, when you were taking antibiotics for that ear infection, did you and Christian use condoms? And don't try telling me that you don't have sex. I'm not an idiot. I've seen the birth control pills." She gestured toward the innocent looking little pink and white packet sitting innocuously next to Sydney's bathroom sink.

Sydney was instantly uncomfortable, feeling as though she was five years old instead of seventeen.

"Since I'm on the pill and we're only with each other... no. We don't use condoms."

She faltered as she saw the glacial look on her mother's face. "I know that's bad, but-"

"Sydney, when was your last period?" Jillian interrupted in a voice that dripped icicles.

Sydney stared at her mother in shock at the implication of the question.

"I don't know. I'm not very regular. It's been a couple of months, I think."

Her mother's face hardened into stone, her mouth a straight, creased line.

Sydney was quick to add, "But that's normal for me. Like I said, I'm not regular. And I'm on the pill. I've never missed taking one."

"You're an idiot, Sydney. How could you be so careless? Antibiotics can negate the effect of the pill. Wait in here. Do *not* come out of this room."

Her mother's voice was so icy, that Sydney didn't bother to assure her that she wasn't going anywhere. She couldn't if she wanted to. She felt too ill to stand up. She simply lay with her cheek pressed pathetically against the floor until her mother returned thirty minutes later.

Sydney sat up shakily as Jillian roughly thrust a small box into her hands, trying to ignore the fact that the room was spinning.

"Here. Take this. I'll wait out here."

Her mother turned her back on her and stalked out without another word.

As Sydney hovered over the toilet, trying to pee on the plastic stick and not her fingers, her sole humorless thought was that wagging her butt over a toilet was definitely not the behavior of a senator's daughter. She sat back down on the cool floor to wait, her head leaned back against the wall and her slender arms wrapped tightly around her knees.

Barely two minutes later, her mother burst back through the door to find Sydney staring in blank fixation at the urine saturated stick in her hand.

"Well?" Jillian demanded impatiently.

Sydney wordlessly turned the pregnancy test toward her.

There were two blue lines.

CHAPTER TWO

Well, today was as good a day as any to die, she supposed. As Sydney glanced around the room, she only saw people that wanted to kill her. Several of them in fact. She might as well be facing a firing squad. Her precarious situation had the same deadly implications.

Even though the Ross family had smiled and acted as though nothing was amiss in front of their photographer, Sydney had needed to duck out and run for the bathroom several times. During one such time, Jillian had taken the liberty of calling Christian's parents. They were now sitting stone-faced next to Christian and across the table from Sydney in her father's den.

Her own parents sat next to the Price's, leaving Sydney to sit all by herself, facing everyone else alone. Right now, she felt as though it was Sydney Ross against the world...the condemned facing the executioner.

Her father's distinguished face was rigid and stern. He alternated between glaring at his daughter and then at the boy who had dishonored her as though he couldn't decide who he was more furious with. Sydney couldn't bring herself to meet his gaze or anyone else's, for that matter.

The tension in the room was palpable. Even Christian was uncharacteristically sober. She felt horrible that she hadn't even been able to tell him the news herself. He kept glancing at her, but his face was so guarded that she had no way of gauging how upset he was. She wondered what he was thinking. Was he angry with her? Was he going to be supportive? She flickered a glance toward him again. He was staring at his hands quietly.

There was no mystery as to where her mother stood, however. She was an open book just like always.

"You stupid little slut!" Jillian's shriek broke the uncomfortable silence. "Couldn't you keep your legs closed?"

"Jillian," her father began, but her mother impatiently cut him off.

"Oh, for God's sake, Randall. Grow a set of balls!" Jillian snapped, before focusing her irritation on Sydney again, her cold eyes glittering with annoyance.

"You're a disgrace!"

Sydney felt tears well up and focused hard on not letting them spill over as she stared at her reflection in the gleaming mahogany table. She looked incredibly pale against the rich hue of the wood. She said a quick silent prayer that she wouldn't throw up in front of everyone. Her stomach was still unstable even though she had nibbled on a handful of crackers.

"She wasn't the only one involved."

Christian's low voice broke through her concentration as he spoke for the first time, braving Jillian's wrath. Sydney raised her head in surprise and met his steady gaze. "I was there, too."

Mrs. Price laid her hand on her son's arm, a clear signal that she wanted him to be silent, but he shrugged it off. Sydney's heart sped up as she realized that he might support her, even though he had been blind-sided with the news. She wished that he would get up and walk around to her side of the table, but he didn't. He continued to sit like a stone next to his parents.

"It doesn't matter. This is a non-issue," Jillian announced matter-of-factly. "I'm going to make an appointment at the clinic for her tomorrow and we'll have it taken care of. Life will go on as normal with no one the wiser."

Sydney's stomach began rapidly sinking and she gulped. She glanced down and saw that her hands were instinctively splayed protectively across her abdomen. Her heart already knew what her mind hadn't registered - she couldn't have it *taken care of.* It was hers and she wanted it. And the only advocate it had… was her.

"Mom, I don't want an abortion." Her voice was so soft that it was almost inaudible and everyone strained to hear her.

Jillian's teeth snapped together as she whipped her perfectly styled head around to stare at her daughter.

"What?"

The single word that Jillian hissed between her teeth resonated throughout the large elaborate room and bounced off of every possible corner. Sydney steeled herself to go head-to-head with her mother. It was an unprecedented event. No one was usually so foolish.

"I don't want to kill my baby. I wouldn't be able to live with myself." Sydney dared a glance at Christian and found him to be just as surprised as everyone else. Her resolve wavered for a brief second at the astounded look on his face.

"Sydney." Christian's expression was puzzled, but still as gentle as his voice. "Syd, you can't keep it. It would ruin everything. Not just for your parents, but for you. And me, too. You're supposed to go to Columbia in a couple of months. I'm going to Princeton. We can't do that pregnant."

She knew he was being logical and smart. But her emotions weren't complying with logic at the moment. She made up her mind, instantly cementing her decision. She couldn't kill it. Her resolve strengthened.

"I know, Chris," she murmured. "And I won't ask you to do anything, I promise. I won't even list you on the birth certificate, if you don't want me to. I'll do everything alone. But I can't kill it. You can't ask me to do that."

"Sydney, you just said it yourself. Right now, it's an *it*. A mass of cells. A nothing. Don't risk our futures for that. Please."

Christian's voice was more subdued than she had ever heard it as he pleaded with her. When she looked into his somber eyes, she recognized the fear that she saw there and her heart broke. For him. Because he hadn't asked for this any more than she had.

"Chris, I mean it. I won't involve you at all. I'll do it myself. It's my decision."

Her voice was barely audible, a mere whisper. She knew that if she spoke any louder, she would cry. She took a deep breath to ward off the tears. It didn't work. She was teetering on the edge of breaking down and it wouldn't take much to make her lose it.

"Princess," her father began, but at Jillian's icy glare, he firmed up his tone.

"Sydney, this isn't only about you. You are not only risking *your* future but also mine and your mother's. And Christian's. You need to think wisely. Please."

His dark brown eyes implored her and she had to look away, staring at the mahogany panels lining the walls instead while a few rebellious tears broke rank and streamed down her cheeks.

"Daddy, I'm sorry. I won't announce to the world that I'm pregnant. I'll be very quiet about it. Maybe it won't raise as much of a stir as you think. Maybe no one will even find out."

Her voice was hopeful and just slightly naïve as she appealed to her father. She was nervously tapping her foot against her chair in a furious cadence, something she didn't even notice as she focused on her father's face.

"Sydney, you know better than that," Randall began, but once again, Jillian cut him off short.

"Sydney, I will not stand aside and let you throw away everything that we've worked for. This is not a request. You will get an abortion. Tomorrow. End of story."

Her mother stood up as she spit the words at Sydney.

Sydney started to answer but was interrupted when Christian's mother spoke for the first time. Until that moment, both she and Mr. Price had been silent, absorbing the conversation but not contributing to it. Now she wasted no time in letting her opinion be known.

"Let's make no mistake. No irresponsible little twit is going to compromise my son's future. I won't allow it. I don't care how much political clout you have or that you have more money than God. I'm sorry, Randall. This isn't personal." The tiny, dark-haired woman looked at Sydney. "You will either get an abortion or you will sign a legal document releasing Christian from any and all ties to that baby. We want no part of this. This whole situation is ridiculous."

"Mom," Christian started to protest.

"Shut up, Christian. You've done enough already. I'm just cleaning up your mess!" his mother snapped.

To Sydney's intense disappointment, he did as his mother demanded and closed his mouth. He sat quietly as everyone else pondered Sydney's future. His eyes held an apology, but it didn't stop Sydney's heart from breaking. The sense of abandonment she felt was stifling.

"Mrs. Price, I'm sorry. I didn't mean for any of this to happen," she murmured, as an errant tear dripped off the end of her nose and landed onto her clasped hands.

"That doesn't change the fact that it *has* happened," Celine Price answered. "And now that it has, you have to do what is best for everyone." Her dark eyes gentled for a brief second before speaking again. "Part of growing up is doing the right thing, Sydney."

"You've been raised to know what the right thing is, Sydney," her mother interjected. "And you will do it tomorrow."

"But mom, this doesn't feel like the 'right thing.' It feels wrong. And I can't be the only one who feels that way. There have been other political daughters who have gotten pregnant and had their babies. Their parents weren't damaged beyond repair. In fact, they were able to spin it in a positive light. They just focused on how their daughters were taking the high road and being responsible."

"Oh, please," Jillian scoffed. "They only chose 'the high road' because they didn't find out early enough to take care of it or because someone else let the information leak to the press. Stop being so naïve."

Talking to her mother was like talking to a brick wall so Sydney once again appealed to her father.

"Daddy, you're against abortion. Everyone knows that. I would think that it would be worse for you if your daughter got an abortion and someone found out, rather than if I had the baby." Her eyes pled with him in earnest and he closed his own for a moment, rubbing his silver tipped temples with manicured fingers before he replied.

"I know, Sydney. I am against abortion. But your mother is right. I've worked too hard to get to where I am to allow myself to become damaged by this scandal. I assure you, no one will find out. The clinic is very discreet. And it's better for you. You have your whole life in front of you right now. You'll have babies when the time is right for you—and that is not right now. Trust me."

She wanted to. But she couldn't. She knew that when it boiled down to it, her parents' top priority was her father's career. Hands down, end of story. Her wants and needs had always been secondary. And it was time that she took them into her own hands because no one else was going to consider them. She took a deep breath and faced her parents with her shoulders back and her chin up.

"Mom... Dad... I'm not getting an abortion. I'm sorry. It's not something I can do. And if you can't accept that then I'm going to have to leave. I won't kill my baby."

She pushed back from the table and glanced at the faces surrounding her, waiting for someone to speak. No one, not even Christian, attempted to stop her. The room was as silent as a tomb.

She fled and flew up the stairs, slamming her heavy door closed and sliding down the length of it until she was a limp heap on the floor. She couldn't stop her tears any longer and sobbed with abandon.

This wasn't the way her life was supposed to be turning out. She was supposed to be carefree and laughing-biding her time until she left for school, where she would party and study for law school in her free time. Her tears continued until they were interrupted by a soft knock on the door a few minutes later.

"Syd?" Christian's low voice was muffled through the thick wooden door.

Sydney scooted to the side before mumbling, "Come in."

The door opened slowly and Christian stepped in, kneeling next to her. Without even looking up, she started crying again and he sank onto the floor, pulling her into his arms. She collapsed weakly against him as she cried, relieved that someone had cared enough to come after her.

"Don't cry, Syd, please. You don't have to do this to yourself."

Christian sounded helpless and uncomfortable as stroked her back soothingly. She tried to get a hold of herself, but her emotions felt like a runaway train. Suddenly, though, a thought occurred to her and she leaned away and gazed up at him with wet lashes.

"Christian, did they send you up here?"

"Well... yes. But I would have come anyway."

He continued patting her back awkwardly, and she knew that he wouldn't have. He was here at his mother's bidding to attempt damage control. To sway her toward reason. She cringed on the inside and any trust that she had in him disintegrated.

"Christian, you might as well go back down and tell them that I'm not changing my mind. I'm sorry." She pushed away from him and stood up, taking a deep, settling breath.

"I'm leaving here and I'm having the baby. But don't worry, I'm not going to ask for anything from you." She was impressed at how steady her voice sounded since she was quite aware that her heart was in tatters.

"Don't be ridiculous. I'll send you money to help. But Sydney, I don't want to be a dad. And I don't want to feel guilty about that. I'm trying to let you know as clearly as I can that I don't want this." His face was rigid as he spoke. "I mean it. I can't do this and I should have a say in this too. I don't want to hurt you because I love you. But I don't want this. I'm sorry."

"Do you? Love me, I mean? Never mind. Don't answer that. I'm sorry, too," she murmured. "It's not like I asked for this, either. But it's here now and I'll deal with it."

She turned her back on him and started packing a suitcase. Her thoughts turned logical as she realized that she should take practical pieces of clothing- ones that she would be able to wear for at least a couple of months while her belly grew. Definitely no skinny pants. She grimaced as she tossed stretchy yoga pants into the suitcase.

"You can go now, Chris."

She didn't even look at him. She didn't relish putting him through this and didn't want to see the anguish on his face. Besides, his face reminded her of a betrayal. A very fresh betrayal.

"Syd…" His voice was pleading as it trailed off. It was clear that he didn't know what to say.

"I mean it. Just go." She forced her voice to be cold so that he would listen.

It was one more moment before she heard the door click shut. She turned to look and Christian was gone. She was all alone. She steeled herself against the pain that instantly ripped through her. She had things to do. She'd let her heart break later.

Before she could think even one more thought, her door flung open again and Jillian Ross walked briskly inside. Sydney decided grimly that the temperature dropped a couple of degrees immediately.

"If you think that we will be helping you, you are vastly mistaken." Jillian's voice was as sharp and unforgiving as barracuda teeth. Sydney didn't even flinch.

"Mom, this is my decision. I don't want anything from you." Sydney didn't look at her mother- she just continued packing, throwing a pair of running shoes into the bag.

"Well, that's good because you won't be getting anything. I'm closing your bank accounts and don't even think about taking your car. I'll report it as stolen if you try.

The title isn't in your name. If this is the path you want to take, take it. But you'll be taking it alone and I'm warning you. It's not going to go well for you. Do not mess with me."

Her mother's steely glare was unwavering and Sydney sucked in her breath. She hadn't expected her mother to be quite so vicious. Angry, yes. Sharp-tongued, yes. Horrendously hateful? No. But then again, she shouldn't have been surprised. Jillian Ross had ice water running through her veins instead of blood. Sydney didn't allow herself to focus on it, though.

She simply said, "I'll be gone in 15 minutes."

Her mother stalked from her room and Sydney was once again alone. She picked up her phone and called a cab and then started feverishly throwing clothing in her suitcase. She added a second suitcase full of toiletries and she stuffed a few sentimental items in there as well, before she took a shaky breath and looked around her.

She was so accustomed to the luxury of her life that she didn't even notice the 1,200 count Egyptian cotton sheets, delicate brushed silk draperies, antique armoire and $10,000 bed. What she saw was the disarray surrounding her- the clothes and personal items scattered everywhere- which she felt was an obvious comparison to her life. Everything was in shattered pieces.

She heard the faint honk of the taxi through her window and she quickly picked up her suitcases, leaving her room without a backward glance. The large foyer was empty as she descended the stairs, so thankfully she didn't have to face anyone. She breathed a quick sigh of relief and quietly left the house without fanfare, putting her bags in the trunk of the cab and then climbing inside.

The burly cab driver grunted, "Where to?"

And she suddenly realized that she didn't know. All she had in the world now were the contents of her two suitcases, the clothes on her back and the money in her wallet which was not a problem that she'd ever had before. She wouldn't be able to live in a hotel very long and she didn't have any relatives.

Except for one.

The idea came to her suddenly. Her distant cousin, Stephen, had found her through a social networking site a year ago and they had been emailing back and forth ever since. He was a writer who was trying to live his dream by writing his first novel. He lived alone and she knew that he would let her stay with him. She pulled out her phone and looked up his address, giving it to the driver.

She leaned back in the smelly cab seat and closed her eyes for the thirty minutes that it took to drive to the South side of Chicago, immersing herself in the gravity of what she had just done. She had literally just given up the life of a princess. And oddly enough, she didn't have any regrets. Of course, it was entirely possible that she might still be in shock.

The sound of the driver locking the car doors made her open her eyes. Pressing her forehead against the window, she immediately understood why. This was far from being a good neighborhood. She could honestly even call it the worst that she had ever been in.

Houses were crammed together like matchsticks. It seemed like there was only an inch or two in between each one. Paint was peeling, trash was in yards. Some had boarded-up windows and some hadn't even bothered...broken glass rose in jagged shards from weathered windowsills. More than a handful looked completely abandoned.

As she took it all in, freshly painted bright red words jumped out at her from the face of one of the dilapidated houses. *SUCK MY DICK, WHORE.* Nice. Painted next to the eloquent words, also in bright red, was a giant sized penis and set of balls. The vandal was also an artist. Definitely not Picasso, but he had gotten his point across.

And Sydney knew it was a *he.* A female would never have painted the penis so large. It had been her limited experience that men always had inflation issues when it came to the perception of their own anatomy. She shook her head. This neighborhood was truly the armpit of the world. But it didn't matter. She didn't have anywhere else to go. She was homeless.

"Miss, are you sure you have the right address?"

The cabbie met her eyes in the rear-view mirror, waiting for a confirmation. If her situation hadn't been so dire, she would have laughed at the puzzlement on his face. As it was, it was so un-funny that it was ridiculous.

"Yes, I'm sure," she confirmed. The cabbie just shook his head as he looked out the window again. It was clear that he thought she was out of her mind.

"I hope so," he commented brusquely. "I've got another call and can't wait for you."

The cab glided up to the curb in front of Stephen's address and she appraised the situation. It didn't look so bad. The little Cape Cod duplex was tiny, but it was neat. The light gray paint looked clean and the grass was freshly mowed. She took a cleansing breath and climbed out of the cab on shaky legs. Her reality was coming down around her ears now and it was leaving her feeling a little weak.

She unloaded her bags, paid the driver and then watched in silence as he drove away. Hopefully, Stephen was home or she was screwed. She was clearly out of place in this neighborhood and people were beginning to stare.

She walked quickly up the sidewalk and pushed the doorbell once. She had never actually met Stephen in person—only online. They had video-chatted, though, so she definitely knew what he looked like. But he certainly wasn't expecting to find her on his doorstep today. She found herself wishing that she had called from the cab. It would have been the polite thing to do but she hadn't been thinking clearly. And she probably still wasn't.

The door opened and Stephen was suddenly facing her, surprise apparent on his strikingly handsome face. He clearly recognized her at once and then his gaze flickered to the suitcases sitting on the porch next to her.

"Sydney?" He phrased her name as a question, as he smiled at her warmly and without hesitation. "Come in."

And she gladly would have. If she hadn't fainted first.

Chapter Three

Time changed everything, Sydney mused as she lay flat on her back on twisted second-hand sheets, running her fingers lightly over her swollen, naked belly. Her slender fingers consciously outlined her fall from grace, tracing every line and growing contour of it. Staring at the dust motes spiraling in the light of the dingy window, she pondered her changed circumstances.

Letting thoughts run rampant, her fingers found a hard lump just below her bottom rib. She pressed on it lightly and her entire belly shifted in reaction. She felt a sudden hard kick against her ribcage and winced.

Her little hitch-hiker was growing stronger by the day. The movements that used to feel like butterfly wings in her belly now felt like shoes tumbling in a dryer. Big, heavy steel-toed work-boots. But she loved feeling the movement anyway. Her baby was growing and thriving, despite so many people who had wanted it dead.

As her hands palmed the ball that was now her stomach, she suddenly felt like an inflated shadow of her normal self. During the past four months that she had been at Stephen's house, she had gained twenty pounds (so far), developed rampant and continuous food cravings and had ankles that swelled up like water balloons in the stifling, suck-the-air-right-out-of-your-body Midwestern heat.

And even though she felt like a bloated, grotesque imitation of herself, the cravings were the worst part because she didn't have enough money to satisfy them anymore.

She definitely hadn't gotten used to the lack of money thing yet. And since she couldn't afford the roasted turkey and hot buttered crab legs that she craved, she consoled herself with cheap replacements like King Size Snickers bars, which did a lot to explain the twenty-pound weight gain.

"Syd?"

A low male voice resonated from the hallway a brief second before Stephen stuck his head through her doorway.

He couldn't really knock because the door itself was long gone, leaving only the protruding painted hinges behind. The gaping rectangular hole left quite a lot to be desired in the privacy department.

"Yes?" she answered quickly, pulling down her shirt.

Her movement stirred the scent of sour milk and sweat. His household was definitely that of a bachelor. She found herself wishing that she could wash the bedding in flower-scented soap, but was afraid it would make her seem ungrateful, like she thought his house wasn't good enough for her. And that wasn't the case.

"Are you going to get up sometime today?"

Stephen's mouth twitched at the corners, although he didn't have any room to talk. Sometimes, when he got a burst of creativity, he would write all night long and then sleep the entire next day.

She sighed delicately, the flush in her cheeks revealing her embarrassment.

"I only meant to lie down for a minute. I've never been so tired in my entire life. The baby steals all of my energy. What time is it anyway?" The way the shadows were slanted against her cramped bedroom walls told her that it was late afternoon.

"It's 4:15. You've been asleep since noon."

The twitch curled into a wide smile. Stephen was the most easy-going person she had ever met. And she loved it when he smiled. It was warm and comfortable, like a favorite pair of jeans.

"You were up by noon to know that?" She eyed him doubtfully.

"Well, Miss Smart-Mouth, maybe not. Maybe you're rubbing off on me!" Stephen winked mischievously as he crossed his arms and leaned on the doorjamb.

He was wearing an old pair of broken-in Levi's that molded to his body and hung off of his hips in the way that only a man's jeans can. He was shirtless, his chest surprisingly toned. She wouldn't have thought that a writer who did no manual labor could be so naturally well-built. But he was. He really could've stepped right out of a Banana Republic catalogue.

He wasn't handsome in the same obvious "look at me" way that Christian was, but he was beautiful in an easy, earthy way. His longish sandy brown hair slanted artistically across his forehead and his dark brown eyes were like melted chocolate. As she stared at him, Sydney felt the need to remind herself of a few key points:

One: He was her cousin. So distantly related that they didn't know exactly how, but family was family.

Two: She was five months pregnant with someone else's baby.

Three: He had taken her in. She was sure that she was simply a charity case to him.

And Four: She was 17 and he was 24. She knew he would never look at her in any way other than friendly.

He was also an alien-creature with strange habits. He was easy-going, laid-back and creative. Three things that Sydney knew very little about.

In her world- well, her *old* world, everyone was driven by schedules, meetings and Blackberries. They were on time for appointments, they went to bed recapping meetings in their heads and they got up the next morning with goals for that day in mind.

In fact, almost everyone she knew had a Ten Year Plan. They were driven to succeed by blinding ambition so that they could maintain their lavish lifestyles. So they could be better than the next guy. They were also superficial, back-stabbing and fake. Stephen was none of these things. It was a refreshing change.

Her stomach suddenly let loose with a loud, unladylike growl. Her hand flew to her stomach as if to muffle it while Stephen laughed. She let the sincere sound of it roll over her like music.

"Sydney, no offense, but you're a bottomless pit. Do you want something to eat?"

It was almost a rhetorical question because she was always, always hungry these days.

"None taken. And do we have anything?"

She only asked because food wasn't important to him. Half of the time he didn't care if he ate or not. He was definitely an eat-to-live kind of guy. She would never utter one word of complaint, though. He had saved her.

"Um, I'm not exactly sure." He seemed to ponder the current state of their typically empty cabinets. "There must be something in there, though. If not, we can go get something."

She had $3.73 in her purse. She knew because she had checked before she went to bed. She would rather not have to spend it on food because she could get an extra-large blueberry slush at the 7-11 for a dollar. As hot as she was, the icy deliciousness of a 44-ounce Big Gulp sounded like Heaven. But her growling stomach reminded her that she definitely needed to eat. The baby needed food. It couldn't thrive on ice and sugar alone.

She shoved her feet into the flip-flops sitting next to her bed. It wasn't hard to choose which shoes to wear anymore. These were the only ones that still fit. She even had to wear them to work. Her tennis shoes cramped her swollen, sausage toes. Thank God it was summer or she would be screwed. She had no idea what she would do when it snowed. She'd just have to cross that bridge when she came to it.

As she attempted to push herself off the bed, Stephen leaned forward with his hand extended. She took it and he hoisted her off the bed with an exaggerated groan. She rolled her eyes. She had only been 103 lbs to start with. So even though she had gained twenty, she still wasn't all that heavy. She only felt like a bowling ball. She didn't look it.

"How are you feeling today?" Stephen asked, giving her the once-over, looking doubtful. He always said that it was hard to tell with her because she never complained.

"I feel good. Why? Don't I look it?" she teased. "Dang! I was planning on entering the Miss America pageant this afternoon! Too much of a stretch?" She grinned widely.

He appeared to consider that for a moment, smiling a little, before he changed the subject.

"Have you heard from your parents?"

He was hesitant, almost cautious.

He didn't usually ask, which was a gesture that Sydney appreciated. It was a sensitive subject and she never, ever brought it up on her own accord. But for whatever reason, maybe to change the subject, he chose to go there now.

"Of course not. Have you?"

She asked the question slightly defiantly, her chin jutting out. She knew that it would be just like them to try to ferret information from him behind her back. The thought pissed her off but she was pretty certain that he wouldn't tell them anything.

"Nope. I'm sure they'll call, though. One of these days."

Stephen was confident. In *his* world, parents didn't turn their backs on their kids. Not permanently, anyway. He just couldn't quite comprehend her world. In hers, mothers said things like *Can't you keep your legs closed, you little slut?*

"It doesn't matter to me if they do. They burned that bridge. Actually, they laced it with C-4 and blew it up." She almost smiled but didn't, trying to be blasé. He was intuitive enough to see through her, however.

He shook his head.

"Don't do that, Sydney. Don't pretend that it doesn't matter and nail shut doors that you might want to reopen someday. I know your parents love you even if they don't show it sometimes." As she stared at him, her expression turned into one of uncontained exasperation. What did he not get?

"Um, Stephen. Do you not remember the day I showed up on your doorstep? Of course you do—I fainted at your feet."

And he had been taking care of her ever since, even if dinner was sometimes cold Spaghettio's from the can. Her heart

suddenly warmed at the thought. Stephen
was a really good man. Gentle and good-
hearted through and through.

And the feelings that she had been
having for him lately were far from cousinly.
She had tried to explain them away to
herself a few weeks ago by pretending that it
was because of her changing hormones. But
the feelings wouldn't go away. She quickly
pushed them out of her mind for the time
being and continued her rant about her
parents.

"What part of my parents trying to force
me to get an abortion paints a picture of
wholesome, unconditional love for you?
Don't believe my father's campaign platform
bullshit for a second. My parents are
definitely not *Family Values First*." Her voice
was cold and adamant. "They aren't going
to call unless I call them first and trust me,
that's not going to happen."

While there was an icy edge to her
voice, even she could hear the painful
undercurrent that flowed heavily under the
surface. And it made her sick that she was
still so affected by her parents' betrayal.

It had been four months since she had
left. Four months without a word from
either of them. They had no idea if she was

in a homeless shelter or on the streets. And if it hadn't been for Stephen, that very well might have been how it turned out.

She had been brushing her hair as they talked and it now fell between them like a thick caramel curtain, hiding her delicate, angular features. As she raised her slender arms to wind it into a knot, the movement stirred her baby within. It reacted with another swift roundhouse kick to her bruised ribs. She cringed in response.

"I disagree. But we'll just have to wait and see, won't we?" Stephen's smile was patient, reflecting the kind man behind it. Reflecting a man who lived in a Mayberry kind of world.

"I wouldn't hold my breath."

She edged past him, something that got significantly harder to do each day, and wandered into the kitchen. She wasn't at the waddling stage yet. She could still walk with dignity. She stretched onto her tiptoes to search through the dingy white cabinets for something to eat.

"Ah-ha!" she announced triumphantly, turning to face Stephen. "Would you rather have chicken noodle soup or beef Ramen noodles?" She held one in each hand.

"Hmm. I'm not sure I like your menu today. What kind of chef are you, anyway?" He grinned cheerfully, unaffected by their slim pickings. "Okay- how about... I take the pasta and you can have the soup de jour?"

"Sounds like a plan. Would you like bread with your meal? Oh, wait. We don't have any."

She rolled her eyes and then smiled to make sure he knew she was only kidding.

"Actually, I think I'm going to walk down to the 7-11 and get a slush before I eat. Do you want to come?"

He shook his head. "Not really...too hot." He raised his eyebrow. "Unless you want me to. But if not, can you bring me one back? Cherry?" He started to pull out his wallet.

"No, no- it's my treat. It's the least I can do." She smiled gently, another subtle Thank You for his hospitality.

"Would you quit that? It's not a problem having you here. I like it, actually. It's the first time in two years that the bathroom has been clean."

The state of his cramped little bathroom when she arrived was enough to make her gag even now. There had even been mold on the shower curtain. Cleaning the house was definitely not a priority for him. His priorities were: Writing, revising and then writing some more. Eating and cleaning were on the bottom of the list as non-essential items.

He was the first creative-type personality that she had ever been around and it was intriguing. He had a habit of dropping everything in order to write when inspiration struck. It didn't matter if he was in the shower or out mowing the grass. But if she found him in the living room writing in his underwear at 2am, it definitely wasn't to get attention. It was simply because he had happened to be undressed when an idea came to him.

Sydney wasn't entirely clear on the process, but apparently, when an idea came along, it could be a very fleeting thing and Stephen needed to grab it while he could. It had taken a little while to get used to his erratic behavior, because her only gauge of male normalcy was her dad. Randall Ross would never be caught dead hanging out in his underwear for any reason.

Her father never even poked his head out of his bedroom in the morning until he was wearing the classic ensemble of the Very

Important Person that he was... perfectly pressed suit, coordinated tie and shoes so highly polished that he could see up his assistant's skirt in them.

Sydney wouldn't know if he wore boxers or briefs to save her life. But he was such a top tier snob that whatever they were, she was positive that they were Christian Dior. It would be unseemly for him to wear anything less than extravagant.

Her cousin, on the other hand, was partial to boxer-briefs. Fruit of the Loom- five pairs for ten bucks. She smiled, remembering the first time she had found Stephen nonchalantly cooking in them as though it was the most normal thing in the world to do. She had stopped dead in the kitchen doorway, not sure where to look. Luckily, she wasn't easily offended and by now she just took his crazy habits in stride.

"What's so funny?" He was watching her face now, trying to read her thoughts.

"Nothing." She shook her head. She would never say anything. He had no inkling that the rest of the world wasn't like him and she wouldn't change a single thing about him.

"I just appreciate everything you've done for me. I'll be back in a few minutes with your slush."

She leaned up and kissed him softly on the cheek before she left. Because her back was to him, she didn't see the color flare across his cheeks.

Their little bungalow didn't have a covered porch so whenever they left the house, they were immediately exposed to the elements. Today, as Sydney stepped onto the front walk, she could feel the sun's intensity slowly easing just a smidge as afternoon began the slow turn into evening.

A breeze kicked up and lifted her bangs off of her face, but even the breeze was hot and didn't provide any real relief. All it did was move around the stagnant heat and the smell of sun-scorched grass. She wished that they had the money to run the air conditioner. She knew it would make a world of difference. It was just one more thing on the long list of things that she used to take for granted.

The kids in the rundown house next door were outside screaming as they took turns hurdling their sprinkler. Their skinny little shoulders were tanned from the sun and they were barefoot as they ran across their brown lawn. It was so dry that it crunched under their feet. It was also unfenced and far too close to the cars that flew by in a blur down the street.

It was clear to her from the drab shade of their grass that their sprinkler was not utilized as a lawn implement. It was strictly for entertainment purposes. But it didn't matter. No one on this street really cared about their lawn, anyway.

It wasn't like her parents' neighborhood where there was an association that regularly measured each lawn to ensure that it was kept a specific length and was the appropriate shade of green. Now that she was out in the real world, she realized the ridiculousness of someone taking the time to walk around another person's lawn with a ruler and color-wheel. There were definitely more important things to worry about in life than that.

"Sydney!" The oldest blonde boy called.

She could never remember his name. It wasn't just the pregnancy hormones messing with her, either. She had never been good with names. People used to mistake it for snobbishness, as though she didn't deem them important enough to put forth the effort to remember. But that wasn't it. She just had a bad memory for things like that.

She would admit, though, that she could spout off the name of every handbag that Coach had ever carried, along with the pattern, color and size of each one. But that was different. That was Coach. Her mom had given her Coach catalogues to look at instead of Dr. Seuss books. But she hadn't bought a new Coach for four months now so it didn't really count anymore.

"Sydney!" The boy called again. Apparently he thought that she hadn't heard him.

She turned and smiled tolerantly at him. The kids were loud, rambunctious and sometimes annoying, but it wasn't their fault. They had no guidance. Their parents left them home alone all day and they got bored. The three of them usually ran like wild little heathens through the neighborhood. This oldest boy couldn't be more than nine or ten. His pale blonde hair hadn't been combed today and he had peanut butter smeared on the corner of his mouth.

"How's the water?" she asked him with a smile, as she inhaled the scent of the fat droplets sizzling on the sidewalk. "It's so hot that I might join you when I get back."

His two little sisters stopped jumping rope in the spray of the sprinkler and stared at her with wide, hopeful eyes.

"Sweet!" he nodded, clearly pleased by the idea that she might play with them. Whatever it was that he had been planning to say had been forgotten with the promise of a potential new friend to play with. She could feel them staring as she continued down the sidewalk. She was pretty sure that they were wondering if she really would come back to play.

She felt a pang of empathy for their situation. It was really pretty sad. They were so hungry for attention that they would take it from whoever would offer it. She hoped that no one ever took advantage of that. Child molesters and other weirdos seemed to have a built-in radar for the kids who were vulnerable. For the ones that would say Yes.

As she walked and thought, she absorbed her surroundings like a sponge, enjoying the shade from the trees lining the sidewalk. This neighborhood was such an alien-planet to her that she never failed to find something interesting every time she went out.

Her experience so far had been that most of the people populating this run-down little place never got out. Stephen was only here because the rent was cheap. His parents were from the North side of town. Not Highland Park like her own, but a nice, suburban area nonetheless. They would gladly help him, but he was independent and didn't want that. She had no doubt that he was going to sell a novel and then leave here. Because any smart person would.

Sydney was suddenly startled out of her reverie as her cell phone buzzed to alert her to a text message. It was her only luxury. She waited tables at the Sunshine Café on the corner to pay for it and even though she was prudent with it now, it took a large chunk of her tip money. She had even downgraded from her Smartphone with the unlimited data plan and it was still an expensive extravagance.

It buzzed again and she pulled it out to read the ten cent message. Apprehension flooded through her when she saw the name. Christian Price.

What R U doing?

She stared at the words. Why did he care? Why now? He hadn't visited her since she had moved out of her parents' house. And he knew where she was- she had texted him to let him know so that he wouldn't worry. She had received no answer, so she had to assume that he didn't care.

None of her former so-called friends had contacted her either which was actually for the best. She didn't have the patience to endure their chirpy, fake platitudes and empty babbling gossip, not now that her life had been changed in such a real way. It had all been very eye-opening. She could clearly see now how fake her prior relationships had all been. She quickly decided to ignore the text. She wasn't going to waste a dime on text message to Christian.

She had no sooner stuck her phone back into her pocket when it rang loudly, vibrating against her leg. Apparently he didn't want to wait for her to answer. God, she hoped he wasn't parked outside of Stephen's house or something.

She gritted her teeth and answered.

"Hi, Christian."

"Hey, Syd." The voice was familiar, but the tone was not one that she had ever heard from him. It was one of resigned, coarse necessity. A vast departure from the sexy charm that he used to use with her.

"I'm calling to see if you need anything." He was quiet and matter-of-fact.

She briefly wondered who he was dating now. The question flitted through her mind before she could stop it, but she would die before she asked him. It wasn't that important to her because he wasn't important to her anymore. It was just idle curiosity, but it rubbed her the wrong way because he was still free to have a life.

"Christian," she mused idly. "Isn't it odd how two people can be involved in the same exact act but only one, the girl, has to pay the consequences?" She wasn't trying to be snotty but the injustice of it all astounded her sometimes. The universe certainly wasn't an equal opportunity employer.

He sighed. "I don't want to hear it, Sydney. This is what you chose. Everyone told you to get rid of it, but you wouldn't. You made your bed." While he wasn't kind, he wasn't unkind either, just brusquely matter-of-fact. And Sydney could hear his parents in every word he said.

"But it wasn't really a choice, was it? Deciding to kill something isn't really something that you can choose. Or at least, I couldn't. And I'm the one that would have had to live with it every day of my life. Not you."

"Whatever, Sydney. No one held a gun to your head. I didn't call for a guilt trip. Do you need anything?"

The agitated sound of his voice filled her with piercing regret. A girl only lost her virginity one time and every girl usually remembered that one boy with perfect clarity- the way he smiled in the dark or stroked her hand or the particular brand of cologne that he wore. And she would remember all of those things.

But in addition to all of those normal things, Sydney was going to have a living reminder of Christian for the rest of her life. And she knew that the only thing he saw when he thought of *her* was a big, fat, binding obligation. It made her sick. She tightened her grip on the phone.

"I'm fine. I don't need anything from you. I've already told you that." Her voice was snippier than she meant for it to be.

"I know. But I told you that I would help so that's what I'm trying to do. Do you need diapers or anything?"

"Christian, it's not even born yet! Why would I need diapers?" She was incredulous. Could he seriously be that clueless?

She walked into the 7-11 as she talked to him, moving directly back to the churning slush machine as they spoke. The ice cold air-conditioning washed over her like a wave, adhering to her slightly damp skin. She inhaled deeply, enjoying the temporary reprieve from the sticky heat.

Maybe this was why she liked walking here for a drink every day. The air-conditioning. It certainly wasn't for the dingy, chipped floors or the company of the hairy guy behind the counter. He had 'Chuck' scrawled on his nametag in faded blue marker. She greeted him every day by name and he had never once asked for hers.

"I don't know. I just thought maybe you wanted to stock up or something."

Christian sounded offended, as though her refusal had hurt his feelings. She sighed. She had to admit that he was living up to his promise and the baby wasn't even here yet.

"Look, I told you. It was my decision to keep it, even though I knew you didn't want to. It's perfectly fine with me if your parents want to draw up papers for you to sign away your rights. Then you wouldn't be legally obligated, either. Send them over to me and I'll sign them. I can raise her myself."

"How, Sydney? You can't earn enough money to live on your own, much less feed a baby and you don't have any job skills. And what about college?" He sounded just like her parents.

For all she knew, they were trying to get information from him, too. That way they could keep tabs on her while still pretending like they didn't care. And maybe they actually didn't anymore. She wasn't sure.

"I'll worry about college later. Right now, I just want to concentrate on having the baby. That's all I can do."

She could practically see him shaking his head through the phone. She had been just like him once- not too long ago. Impatient, entitled and slightly self-absorbed. It really wasn't his fault, it was just a by-product of their upbringing. But she realized now that she didn't know anything back when she was like him.

"I need to go, okay? My hands are full. I'll talk to you later." She flipped her phone closed and carried the two giant slippery cups to the counter to pay for them.

"$2.11," Chuck grunted.

That was it, not another word. No Please, Thank-you or Come Again. Of course, he knew that she would. Come Again. Every day that she had enough money, she came. It was the only thing she could do to treat herself. She didn't have enough money anymore for a massage or a mud wrap.

She had $1.62 left, which was more than enough to buy the neighbor kids some snow cones. They were only a quarter each at the little Dairy Barn down the street. Not many people were nice to those kids. No one else saw past the annoyance of their noise.

Besides, she knew that when she went to work tomorrow night, she would replenish her stash with tips. On a normal weekday, she usually made 20 or 30 bucks. People felt sorry for the pregnant young waitress with the swollen, Herman Munster feet.

Juggling the oversized cups carefully, she pushed the cool glass door open with her hip and stepped out into the sun, squinting into the bright light. It was always such a drastic difference walking from the cold interior of the building into the sun beating down on the scorching concrete. She took a second to acclimate herself to breathing the muggy air again. It was so humid that it was like inhaling a glass of water.

She had only taken a few short steps before the loud revving of an engine and the sound of squealing tires commanded her attention. She turned to locate the source of the noise but barely had time to register the smell of burning rubber or to focus on the car tearing into the parking lot before it hit her. The old black Trans-Am drove straight into her as though it was on a zip-line attached to her chest. As though it had purpose.

The impact threw her forcefully against the bricks of the convenience store wall before she slid limply to the ground, her legs splayed around her and her Big Gulp cups splattered onto the hot pavement. As her eyes fluttered closed, she saw the battered car back up and spin around, speeding back in the direction that it had come from. And then nothing.

Chapter Four

If she had seemed delicate before with her swollen little belly and bird-like arms and legs, then she was excruciatingly fragile now. She was beyond pale. Every drop of blood had leached from her face until she almost blended into the white blanket beneath her. The dark fringe of her closed eyelashes was striking in contrast with the pale cheeks that they rested against.

Everything hurt. She couldn't get away from it. All around her- up, down, right, left... there was pain. It raged from the tips of her fingers to the arches of her feet. Her stomach was spasming uncontrollably, wrapping around to convulse in her back. It was so excruciating that it stole the breath she was trying to take. She knew there was a lot of blood. She could feel it gushing between her legs. Her face was also wet but she wasn't sure if it was tears or blood. And she was afraid to open her eyes to find out.

She wasn't dead. She knew that because there was a siren wailing in the background somewhere. And surely there weren't any sirens in Heaven. Or pain. She took a deep breath and it smelled strange, medicinal. She struggled to open her eyes and it took her a second to realize that there was an oxygen mask strapped to her face. She raised her hand to pull at it and someone gently pushed it back down.

"No, sweetie. You need that. Leave it be."

A fuzzy female face blurred back out of her vision, but Sydney felt the person moving beside her. Poking, prodding. They were moving. She focused harder. There were medical supplies hanging from the walls and she was strapped to a gurney. She was in the back of an ambulance. She definitely wasn't dead.

But what about her baby?

She yanked off the mask before the woman could stop her.

"Is my baby okay?" she asked urgently. Her voice was hoarse. Her throat felt gummy and she didn't know why. She could taste the metallic, rusty flavor of blood on her tongue.

Another wave of pain wracked her body and she curled upward as she tried to absorb it, to cushion it. It didn't work. She couldn't breathe and the oxygen wasn't helping. She fought to inhale so that she could scream.

The kind female face hovered over her, replacing her mask and holding her arm tightly. There was a quick pinch and then warmth spread through her body. Everything blurred into nothingness.

* * *

"Syd?"

Sydney opened her eyes to stare at a blank white wall. She struggled to focus, to figure out what had happened. The oxygen mask was gone and so was the pain. Well, the excruciating pain, anyway. She could deal with the piercing aches that she felt now. Her hands immediately flew to her stomach. It was flat, in an unbaked dough kind of way. Empty.

She turned her head to find Stephen's face. He was sitting in a chair pulled up right next to her bed, her small hand clasped in both of his. Her fingers were ice cold, his were warm. They were alone in a hospital room. Blank walls, white floor. The sterility was smothering.

"The baby?" she whispered, afraid to know.

But it was the one thing she had to know, the only thing that mattered. She didn't care if she had lost a foot, broken ten bones or had snapped her spine. Her baby's life was her sole focus.

He looked away as he shook his head, not knowing how to say it. The look on his face was enough. Crushing sorrow bowed her shoulders with its weight and she closed her eyes as her heart silently broke into pieces.

"I'm so sorry, Syd. They did everything they could. You're lucky to be alive, that it didn't rupture your liver. One of your lungs collapsed."

Her arm brushed against a tube connected to her chest. Milky, reddish fluid dripped from her lungs through the tube and into a plastic bag hanging on the side of her bed. The severity of her situation began to dawn on her.

"What happened?" she whispered.

The details were foggy. She remembered a beat-up black car and that was pretty much it. She hadn't even been in the street. She had just barely stepped out of the 7-11.

"You don't remember? Someone plowed into you and then drove away. The police were already here. They're going to check the surveillance footage from the convenience store to try to identify the guy." He squeezed her hand lightly. "They're going to come back to talk with you.

"Sydney, I'm so sorry that I didn't go with you. Maybe if I had…"

His voice trailed off and he looked down at his hands, his chocolate brown eyes tortured with regret and guilt. Sydney shook her head. It wasn't his fault. But she would have to address that later.

Right now she needed proof, because she couldn't quite wrap her head around her loss without it. The last time she had opened her eyes from sleep, her baby had been healthy and kicking, bruising her ribs with every movement. She couldn't go from that to this without seeing the evidence.

"Where's my baby? I need to see her."

Her voice was soft but firm even though every word she spoke rasped against her tender broken ribs like a scalpel.

She knew beyond any doubt that it had been a girl. She had known that from the moment she took the pregnancy test. She had also known that she was going to name her Aspen Nicole. That name just seemed to match the perfect little face that she had already seen in her head a hundred times. Her sense of loss was all-consuming and she tried to steel herself against it.

Stephen looked away, again uncertain how to respond.

"Stephen?"

She didn't need to ask the question again.

For the second time that day, Stephen had to apologize for things that were out of his control. He fiddled with the edge of her blanket, apparently unsure what to do with his hands. He finally settled for picking up her hand again.

"Sydney, she's gone. I'm so sorry. Your parents were here for a little while to sign all of the papers. Your mother told the nurses to dispose of her." He couldn't hold her gaze and she stared at his sympathetic face.

To. Dispose. Of. Her.

A lead weight sprung up in her stomach and pinned her to the bed. She fought back nausea as pain welled up from her stomach into her throat in the form of acidic bile.

They had thrown her baby out with the garbage and then they just signed the necessary paperwork and left. Before anyone saw them, she was sure. And they hadn't even waited for her to wake up. She wondered if Stephen was so firm in his convictions that they loved her now.

"Did they even look at her?" she asked thinly, although she knew the answer before he shook his head.

Of course they hadn't. To them, she was just a mass of cells, a problem. If they looked at her, they would have to acknowledge her...to acknowledge that she had little hands and feet. They wouldn't do that. So no one had seen her baby- the little face that she had waited for months to see.

Sydney's pain was overwhelming and she was on the verge of losing it... of snapping, screaming, thrashing, throwing things. She took a deep breath, then another, willing her shuddering lungs to calm. Finally, she leveled her gaze at her cousin.

"She was a girl, wasn't she?"

Her voice was deadly calm and oh-so-frail and Stephen nodded slowly, assessing her face. She showed no outward signs of distress, but anyone who knew her at all knew that it was a façade. Something she had 17 years practice at perfecting.

Stephen squeezed her hand gently because there was nothing he could say right now that would help. He knew that and so did she. Sydney laid her free hand on her hollow stomach and lay perfectly still, listening to the clock on the wall tick past the seconds as she stared listlessly at the wall. Words would be a distraction. She only wanted to think.

An hour passed as they sat in silence, with only the beeping of the hospital machines and the muted thudding of the nurses' shoes in the hallway for noise. Time did not register with her. She was cognizant only of trying to repress the waves of pain and shock, to tuck it into the furthermost corner of her consciousness into a safe place. A place that wouldn't hurt her.

The more still she became, the more she was able to empty her mind and think of nothing. It was numbing like anesthesia. So she found a spot on the wall and fixated on it, breathing deeply in and out, as if she were meditating.

On the outside, it wasn't apparent that she was desperately clinging to the last vestiges of her sanity. But she was. And Stephen quietly held her hand, not saying a word, giving her exactly what she needed. Silent support.

Later, when she recalled that day, Sydney would be able to pinpoint that it was at that exact moment that she fell in love with him...her distant cousin with the friendly eyes and the gentle hands. But she was too immersed in the moment to recognize it at the time. Too overwhelmed trying to survive the pain.

She eventually drifted off to sleep. It seemed like a good idea to escape her new reality. The nurse had come in to give her another pain shot and the drowsiness overtook her like a current in the ocean. She allowed her eyes to close and she drifted away on it, but she still held Stephen's hand tightly. She silently willed him not to leave...to stay with her. She had never felt so alone in her life.

Stephen was still watching her sleep when the police returned to interview her an hour later. They knocked briefly on the door, two quick raps, before they went ahead and entered. Sydney stirred from her drug-induced rest as she heard the voices next to her bed.

"Ms. Ross?"

The man standing in front of her, Detective Harrison Daniels, possessed a commanding attitude, one of curt formality. He was not the type of person that Sydney would have imagined as a detective.

He was tall, dark-haired and had the look of a Wall Street investment banker, not a policeman. His fingernails were manicured, his clothing expensive. His gaze was intelligent as his discerning eyes scanned the room. He took everything in- the lack of visitors, the absence of flowers, Stephen's hands holding hers, everything. It made Sydney feel self-conscious and she pulled her hand from Stephen's before she answered.

"Yes?"

"I'm Detective Daniels. This is my partner, Detective Wills. We'd like to ask you a few questions about your accident."

He spoke in a decisive manner as he motioned to his partner, who was a short, hard-faced woman with pinched lips. Her hair style was as sensible as her black walking shoes. She wore very little makeup and her fingernails were unkempt. It was clear that she didn't take much time for personal pampering although Sydney could tell from her muscled biceps that she must spend hours in the gym.

"Of course. But I don't remember much."

Sydney was already apologetic. She knew she wasn't going to be much help. Her memory was sketchy at best.

"Anything that you can remember will be helpful."

The detective dismissed her statement with cynical disregard as though her opinion was of the most miniscule of importance. It was clear that he felt that he was the only one qualified to determine what was helpful and what was not.

Sydney was immediately taken aback by the curtness in his voice which only served to put her on edge. His partner moved around the bed to stand closer to Sydney, pulling out a little leather notebook and a heavy ink pen.

"What do you remember, Ms. Ross?"

Detective Wills had the no-nonsense manner that Sydney would have expected from a detective as well as the dumpy clothes and the coffee breath. She could tell from her burned out demeanor that this woman was someone who had seen everything and had probably spoken with a hundred girls just like Sydney. And it was very apparent that she was weary of it.

Stephen picked up her hand again reassuringly. She didn't pull away this time even though Detective Daniels flickered his gaze briefly as he registered the gesture. Sydney tried not to care because they weren't doing anything wrong. The warmth of Stephen's hand gave her the assurance that someone in the room was on her side. The unexpected glacial cold emanating from Detective Daniels certainly wasn't doing it for her.

"I only remember an old beat-up car. It was black. And it had a big gold bird on the hood. I didn't see it at all before it hit me, only when it was backing up to drive away. And there was the smell... burning rubber, I think. I heard tires squealing."

"You didn't see the driver when he struck you?" Detective Wills' pen hesitated on her paper, waiting for Sydney to confirm.

"No. I didn't. It happened too fast. I heard a loud engine and the next thing I knew, I was on the ground. I didn't even feel anything at the time." The heavy pen scratched quickly against the paper.

"Were the car windows up or down?"

"I don't know."

"Were the windows tinted?"

"I don't know."

"Was the car in the parking lot when you went into the store?"

"I don't think so. But I didn't notice."

"Do you know anyone with a black Trans-Am or Firebird?"

"No."

"Do you know anyone who would want to hurt you?"

The pen lingered over the paper, waiting for something to write.

Sydney halted her answers and stared at the detective in shock. She had been under the assumption that it was a strange, random accident. The idea that someone had tried to kill her dawned on her as suddenly as someone dumping ice water on her head.

"You think someone hit me on purpose?" she asked incredulously. "Who would do that?"

"That's what we're trying to ascertain, Ms. Ross. Do you have any ideas?"

"Why would you think they did it on purpose?" She couldn't wrap her mind around the fact that someone would want to hurt her enough to ponder who it could be.

"The clerk in the store saw a late model black Trans-Am speeding into the parking lot, as though it had been waiting for you to walk out of the store. It hit you then made a quick three-point turn to escape from the parking lot. Unfortunately, the glare of the sun was on the windshield so he couldn't get a description of the driver. He couldn't see the tag either because the driver fled the scene too fast. But they're pulling up the surveillance tapes for our review. Do you have any enemies?"

"No. I don't. I mean, my ex-boyfriend's parents hate me because I got pregnant. But I don't think I would call them enemies. They just pretend that I don't exist."

"When is the last time that you spoke with them?"

"When we told them that I was pregnant... about four months ago."

When Mrs. Price called had called her a stupid little twit.

"How did they take the news?"

"Not well. They wanted me to get an abortion."

"Why didn't you?"

Stephen interrupted, surprise and annoyance on his handsome face. "What does that have to do with the situation? Is it relevant?"

"Yes, it is. I am trying to determine Ms. Ross' motives." Detective Wills barely spared him a glance before turning her attention back to Sydney. "Were you hoping to get money from them?"

Shock rippled through Sydney again. Why in the world would she want to get money from them? That had been the furthest thing from her mind.

Stephen interrupted again. "This is ridiculous! Of course she wasn't. Do you realize who her parents are?"

He unconsciously moved closer to Sydney, a move that he didn't even realize but that Detective Daniels certainly did. The detective absorbed everything, his face impassive.

Sydney squeezed his hand. "It's okay, Stephen."

The detective's eyes continued their cold appraisal. He filed away Stephen's protective demeanor in his mind as he watched their gentle interaction.

"You've already spoken with the Prices', haven't you?" she softly asked. "I can tell that you have. They don't like me much. But I don't want their money. I just couldn't get an abortion, that's all. I wanted the baby.

They should be happy now, though. She's gone."

Sydney closed her stinging eyes, a sudden weariness flooding over her even though she had just woken up. Stephen shifted his gaze from her to the detectives.

"Will that be all? Sydney's been through a lot. She's tired."

Stephen's voice was firm. His question wasn't really a question at all; it was a statement that the interview was over. Detective Daniel, however, made it clear that it would be over when he said it was over. He stepped closer to them, his eyes glinting firmly as he gazed at the two of them.

"We're just trying to do a thorough job, Mr. James. We have to understand everyone's motives so that we can find out who did this." Detective Daniels' steel blue eyes stared at Sydney, his voice no longer perfunctory; instead it was cold and penetrating.

"Why would someone with the world on a string choose to get disinherited for a surprise pregnancy? You just graduated high school and are not married. You weren't even in a relationship. It would seem to me that the easiest thing to do would have been to get rid of it and go on with your life. Unless you wanted something." He continued to stare at her, unflinching.

"What exactly are you insinuating? I thought you were trying to find out who tried to kill Sydney. But it seems as though she is on trial here. Why is that?" Stephen's voice was hard and his eyes sparked as they locked with the iron gaze of the detective.

Sydney stared at him in shock. This hard assertiveness was not a side of Stephen that she had seen. It didn't match his easy-going personality but she found that it didn't trouble her. It actually had just the opposite effect. She felt protected. For the first time in her life, someone was standing up for her.

"We're just doing our job. We have to understand the dynamics of this situation so that we can figure out who did it and why. For instance, we need to know if Ms. Ross was trying to get money from the Prices' so that she could run away with you."

Even though he was speaking to Stephen, Detective Daniels' gaze was locked on Sydney to gauge her reaction as her eyes flew to him in surprise.

"This has nothing to do with Stephen! We only casually knew each other when this whole thing happened. He was nice enough to take me in when my parents kicked me out. Instead of trying to smear me, why aren't you more focused on finding out who did this? I'm the victim here, not the Prices'."

Sydney was frustrated now and her fragile emotional state shone through loud and clear.

"I don't believe this! Somebody ran me down and killed my baby and you are treating me like a criminal! I didn't do anything wrong!" Her hands started shaking as she spoke, shock lodging deeply in her chest at the turn of events in this interrogation.

"We're sorry for upsetting you, Sydney. We just have to know everything so that we *can* figure out who did this. We'll let you know what we find out and if we need to speak with you again."

Stephen stared at him. "Do that. And maybe next time you can be a little kinder. This girl has just lost her baby."

Stephen didn't even bother looking at them again as he turned his attention back to Sydney. He had never seen anyone look so vulnerable. Her wide eyes were full of bleak loneliness and she seemed lost...like she had been somewhere that he could never, ever go. Stephen felt protective urges twinge inside of him that he'd never felt before. Sydney seemed so small as she lay wrapped in tubes and tape.

Both detectives turned their backs without another word and walked out, taking their blatant discourse with them and closing the door behind them. Sydney looked at Stephen in confusion.

"What is going on?" Her jeweled eyes glistened as though she was going to burst into tears at any moment.

"Don't worry about it, Syd. You didn't do anything wrong. I'm a big believer that truth always comes out so they'll figure it out. Eventually."

"But why were they treating me like a criminal?"

Her soft voice wavered. Stephen brushed the hair out of her face and then rubbed her arm comfortingly.

"Because they already spoke with the Prices' and your parents. I'm sure it was the impression that they received from them. Don't waste your time thinking about it. You just focus on getting some rest, okay?"

Sydney shook her head. It was going to be hard to rest with all of the thoughts that were swirling around in her head. The turn of events was unbelievable. She had gone from being a victim of a hit and run to finding out that it was probably a planned attack to being interrogated like a criminal. She was pretty sure she wouldn't be sleeping for awhile.

She was asleep five minutes later.

Stephen stayed with her as she slept; watching her sleep, reading magazines, pacing the floor. He sat by her bed like a sentinel, guarding her as she slept although no one came back to bother her except for the nurses who took her vital signs every hour. She slept like the dead.

He kept his bedside vigil as the hours turned into days. He barely left her side to shower or eat although she frequently encouraged him to go home and get some rest. He refused. Stephen was used to erratic schedules. And he was her sole visitor. There was no way he was going to leave her alone in the sterile hospital room with only the scent of Lysol and overworked nurses to keep her company.

Finally, six days later, Sydney was discharged from the hospital with orders to rest at home and a prescription for birth control pills. As they rolled down the road in

Stephen's black vintage T-Bird, he laid her cell phone in her lap. She was surprised to realize that she hadn't even missed it for the week that she was in the hospital.

She opened it now to check her messages. There was only one. Holding her breath, she opened her phone to find that the text was from Christian, not her parents.

She exhaled slowly, letting her warm breath escape in a thin rush over her lips. She had no idea why she had thought that they might show concern now or why she allowed herself to feel disappointment that they didn't. It shouldn't be a surprise. They had left her in the hospital without seeing her. They had to know that she was going to be devastated.

I'm sorry.

The two stark words screamed at her from the small screen.

Christian had spent two seconds typing a two-word message. Their baby had died and he was *sorry*. But he wasn't really, she knew that. He was relieved. He wasn't going to have a kid running around that he would never even know. The fact that he couldn't even bring himself to ask how she was doing echoed over and over in her head.

She couldn't believe that she had wasted her virginity on him.

Stephen reached over and wrapped his arm around her shoulders as he drove and she dropped her head onto his broad shoulder. As she stared absently at the scenery blurring past, she decided that the best thing to do was to try and file away her pain like a memory. Tucking it away in the farthest recesses of her mind, hiding it from herself, seemed like the smartest thing to do.

The ride home passed in peaceful silence. When they pulled up to the house, Stephen unloaded her bag from the trunk and helped her walk inside. She suddenly felt like a cripple as she hunched over her injuries and hobbled into the house. As Stephen grasped her elbow, she turned to him with a smile.

"I'm not an invalid, Stephen. I'm feeling much better. My ribs are barely even sore now. Just don't make me laugh."

She smiled again convincingly and followed Stephen as he walked toward her bedroom. As they walked down the short hall, she gasped. A freshly painted door was hanging in her doorway. He barely even glanced at it as he opened it nonchalantly and waited for her to enter first. She gasped again.

Her room had a fresh coat of Robin's Egg blue paint on the walls, her favorite color. The bed in the center of the back wall had a new white eyelet bedspread, turned down at the top, topped with plump new pillows. She could see fresh new linens poking out from underneath. A lacy white throw was folded at the foot. She turned to Stephen, shock apparent on her face.

"What?" he asked innocently, as he set her bag beside her refurbished bed. A small, self-satisfied smile tilted the corners of his lips.

She looked around again in dumbfounded amazement.

"How did you...?" She couldn't seem to form a cohesive sentence.

This act of kindness had taken her completely off-guard. It was ironic to her that once upon a time, she had the bedroom of a princess and hadn't thought twice about it. The thoughtfulness behind this tiny, simple redecorated room touched her more deeply than her old king-sized bedroom suite ever had.

"I thought it might make you smile." It was his turn to shrug lightly.

"But how did you find time? You were with me almost every minute!" Her eyes were wide as she stared at him.

"I do what every un-married male does when he needs help. I called my mom."

He grinned widely as she continued to examine her new surroundings. Her clothing was folded neatly on a stack of new dark wicker shelves in the corner. There were even a couple of framed still-life prints hanging above the bed and crisp white eyelet curtains to match the bedspread. The crudded-over window had been washed and sparkled in the sun.

The room had definitely felt a woman's touch. Sydney felt a surge of gratitude for the distant relative that she had never even met. Stephen's mother had clearly spent hours redecorating this space for her.

"I'm sorry that I didn't think of it before. I'm a guy. I just don't think of things like that. But I called my mom to ask her what might cheer you up and she took over. Do you like it? Is it okay?" He eyed her anxiously, not sure if she would be upset that he had invaded her personal space.

She rushed to him and hugged him as tightly as her wounded ribs would allow.

"Stephen, this is literally the sweetest thing that anyone has ever done for me. Ever."

She hugged him again, ignoring the protesting twinges that came from her ribs.

"Thank you so much! This is the most thoughtful birthday present anyone has ever given me!" Her eyes shone and he stared at her in shock.

"Your birthday?"

Color flooded his cheeks as he spoke. She nodded in response.

"Sydney, I'm so sorry- I had no idea!"

Sydney studied him curiously for the source of his embarrassment. He had no way of knowing that it was her birthday. He also couldn't know that the first thought that sprung into her mind this morning was the fact that she was another year older now. She was 18. And that meant that being attracted to Stephen didn't feel quite so criminal.

"It's alright," she murmured gently. "How could you know? I didn't tell you. But this is perfect. You couldn't have done better even if you had known." She sat gingerly on the bed, enjoying the lush softness of her new down comforter.

"Syd, you're moving pretty slow. I know you're hurting worse than you're letting on. Let's get you settled into bed. The doctor said you needed to rest, so that's what you're going to do. Are you hungry? I'm going to get you settled in here and then I'll make you something to eat." He hadn't even waited for her answer before he moved her bag out of the way and started turning down her bedding.

"Sydney?" He looked at her questioningly.

"Um, I'd be a lot more comfortable in my nightgown but it hurts to raise my arms over my head." At his concerned look, she quickly added, "But that's really the only thing that hurts. Everything else is just an ache. No big deal."

"Right. Broken ribs and a collapsed lung are no big deal."

He stared at her in amusement. She knew that she was stubborn in her efforts to pretend that she was fine, but she was also well aware that it was in Stephen's nature to worry. She'd given him enough to worry about lately and hurried to reassure him again.

"They really aren't a big deal. They healed up quickly. They must be healed- the doctor took the tape off of them yesterday. They only ache when I move wrong." He couldn't say anything to that and she knew it.

He sighed in resignation. "What do you want me to do?"

"Well, it would be great if you could help me maneuver my nightgown so that I can slip into it." She looked at him hopefully.

"Um, sure. I can do that."

He stared at her hesitantly, his thoughts unreadable. If she didn't know better, she would think that he didn't want her to take her shirt off. And she had to admit... being in such cramped quarters with him while she was taking off her clothes wasn't going to help put a damper on the attraction that she was trying hard to ignore.

She sifted through the clothing in her hospital bag and found the thin gown that she was hunting for. She held it out to him, hoping that he wouldn't notice the slight tremor in her hand.

He took it from her and stepped closer.

"So, how do you want me to go about this?" He looked from the gown to her in such consternation that she burst out laughing and then had to hold her ribs.

"Ow, ow." She gasped, still laughing. "Don't make me laugh."

"I didn't mean to." He gazed at her in such droll amusement that she had to laugh again.

"Oh, God. Stop. It hurts." She wrapped her arms around her body and tried to still the quakes of amusement that threatened to erupt into laughter. Every time she looked at him, the humor bubbled up again. She couldn't help it. He looked so helpless holding her nightgown in his long masculine fingers.

"Okay." She took a deep breath, quelling the remnants of laughter. "If you can help me slide my shirt off and then help me ease my nightgown on over my head, it would be extremely helpful. I can show you how the nurse and I did it this morning."

He held her nightgown out helplessly and she burst into laughter again.

"At this rate, I'm going to need more pain pills," she sighed after the laughing fit had subsided. "Okay, let's try this again." Stephen remained silent, afraid that anything he said would make her laugh and cause her pain again.

Sydney shrugged her arms out of her shirt and he lunged forward to help. He grabbed the back of her collar and tugged it up over her head as she bent over to slide it off. As gentle as Stephen tried to be, it still hurt. A second later, she stood in front of him in only her lacy white bra and he stood with her shirt hanging limply in his hands.

She dared a glance into the mirror hanging over the battered dresser, flinching as she came face-to-face with her unpregnant body. She had become accustomed to her swelling belly and the absence of it was a shock, causing her to gulp hard. Large yellowish-blue bruises adorned most of her torso like an abstract painting. She was a walking bruise.

She was also surprised by her silhouette. She had thought that she would be plumper than she was but she hadn't been hungry lately and it had clearly taken a toll on her. The twenty pounds in baby weight appeared to be gone and through the mottled bruising, she could clearly see her ribs.

"God, Sydney." Stephen stared at her in sympathy, his eyes taking in her battered appearance. "You need to rest."

Sydney noted that to his complete credit, Stephen's eyes didn't even flicker down to her chest and to the way the top of her breasts were peeking out from her bra.

He was a complete gentleman through and through. She was too tired to worry that maybe he just wasn't interested in looking.

As carefully as he could, he helped her ease into her nightgown, pulling it over her head and tugging it down to cover the rest of her bruised body. She sank gently onto the bed and carefully leaned back onto the pillows, closing her eyes.

"I didn't realize how tired I actually am," she sighed.

Stephen slipped from the room to grab a 7-Up for her from the kitchen. He knew that she didn't have the stomach flu but it just seemed like a logical thing to do. He poured it into a glass and stuck a straw in it before he carried it back to her room.

She was already asleep. Stephen gazed at her for a moment longer before he backed quietly out, closing the newly hung door softly behind him.

CHAPTER FIVE

A year or two ago, a biographer had approached her father, wanting to document his rise to power, wanting to put to paper the years leading up to the Randall Ross that the world knew now.

Senator Ross had declined. Graciously, of course, because it wouldn't do to give the impression that they weren't grateful for public interest and support but it was still a decline, nonetheless. He had privately told Sydney and her mother that he wanted to wait until he had become president. Yes, he was just that ambitious and confident.

Sydney rifled through photos in the small box that she had brought with her when she moved. It had been carefully sealed with gray utility tape until today, marked 'Sentimental Items' with a thick black marker. She had always been the kind of girl who kept flowers from dances, love notes from old boyfriends and ticket stubs from great movies.

She used to stick them in little ornamental jeweled boxes that her father would bring home from business trips or the big heavy ornate chest that she had gotten as a gift from the Ambassador to India. When she had left that day five months ago, she had hurriedly taken a few handfuls of these memories and shoved them in a plain cardboard box. They were all she had now.

Everything from her prior life was documented with pictures. She used to insist on it. Her life was a fairy tale, right? There was no reason not to freeze each moment in time so that she could look upon it later and smile.

In the ones scattered in her lap, her parents smiled the same picture-perfect fake smiles, a beautiful blonde Barbie and a charismatic dark-haired Ken. Barbie always had her head turned a certain way, in what she knew was her most flattering pose. Ken had silver at his temples, but was still a handsome, elegant man with power radiating from his ultra-white politician's smile and sincere brown eyes.

Looking at her parents caused Sydney to cringe. It was hard for her to remember her previous life. For the past months since she had left them behind, she had felt like a ghost... someone who had died and no one, especially not her parents, could see. And now, for the two weeks since she had left the hospital, she had been living in a tattered, dinged up corner of her consciousness... the place least damaged from her loss, from her life, from her reality.

Stephen had been her savior, her guardian. He had turned into her best friend and had let her wander in her parallel universe with only gentle admonitions to eat or to rest. He hadn't imposed, advised, judged or instructed. He had simply allowed her to immerse herself in quiet grief and silent reflection. He instinctively knew that it was what she needed to recover. And it was. Today, for the first time, she felt like a living person again.

Loud, staccato knocking dragged Sydney back into the present. She knew she had to answer it because Stephen was out. She padded lightly into the living room, clad only in a t-shirt and running shorts. She opened the door to find the unpleasant presence of Detectives Wills and Daniels on their doorstep. It was also unexpected. She hadn't spoken with them since their rude interview at the hospital.

"We're sorry. Did we wake you?" Detective Daniels' face was impassive, but he didn't sound sorry. Or even slightly concerned.

"No. May I help you?" she asked coolly.

During the past couple of weeks, she had more than enough time to consider the way they had treated her and she didn't appreciate it. It didn't matter who her parents were or weren't, no one should be treated that way in the midst of a crisis. Now was as good a time for any for her breeding to rear its head.

"We have a few more questions for you… about your accident."

"Clearly, I assumed it was about my accident. I'm not in the habit of meeting with the police otherwise." Sydney tilted her head back slightly, sticking her nose in the air, purveying them as though they were idiots.

Detective Daniels' raised a dark eyebrow. "Hmm. Someone ran out of milk for her cereal this morning."

"No, someone just had time to consider the way certain detectives treated her last time and *someone* doesn't appreciate it."

Her tone exhibited every ounce of rich girl breeding that she could muster. Cool, unflappable, superior. It wasn't how she felt but there was no way they could know that. She had years of practice at exhibiting her public persona.

"Please, won't you come in?" Exercising that practice, she was the polite hostess now, swinging the door wide open and gesturing with her arm. "Have a seat." Polite as she was, her voice was still cool.

They both looked around the room with the practiced observation of detectives, taking in the scant furnishings, bare walls, small television, scruffy oak desk piled with paper in the corner and a hibernating laptop screen. The sheer curtains framing the open windows fluttered in the hot breeze, accentuating the lack of air-conditioning.

She knew that the room screamed Minimal Living but it didn't concern her and neither did their opinion of it. She had spent the earlier morning hours scrubbing the worn wooden floors until they shone. The little house might not be fancy but it was lemon-scented and clean.

"We'll stand, thanks."

Detective Wills once again pulled out her little pad of paper as she stood in place, rocking back and forth on her heels.

"Ms. Ross, we're not your enemies here. We're simply trying to answer the question of who tried to kill you. Any help you can give us furthers that cause."

The detective's voice was sincere even if it did lack warmth. Sydney briefly wondered if she was a lesbian. Normal women didn't have such large biceps. Not that she cared about the woman's sexual orientation, because she didn't.

But she did have to concede that the detective was right. She was only hurting herself by making an enemy out of the police. Even if she did feel that they had been influenced by her parents.

"Okay," she answered flatly. "I'll try to remember as much as I can. But honestly, it's just not there for me to recall. It happened so fast that I really didn't see anything."

Detective Daniels' stepped forward. "Actually, we're not here to ask about your accident. We're here to ask you some questions about your relationship with Christian Price."

Surprise filtered through her although she didn't know why. She should be used to it, at any rate. She had been surprised a hundred times in the past six months. Beginning with her pregnancy. That had been a big one. This was nothing compared to that.

"Christian? What about him? We dated for a few months. Obviously, we had a sexual relationship. I've known him since grade school. He didn't want to be a dad so we broke up."

"How long would you say your relationship lasted? Exactly." Detective Daniels' bright blue eyes studied her carefully, interested in her answer.

"Well, let's see." Sydney counted in her head. "I guess maybe six months or so. Maybe a little less."

"Well, see, that's where we're confused. Mr. Price stated that you didn't have an actual relationship, that you both got drunk at a party and had sexual intercourse one time."

"What? That's a lie. Why would he say that? We dated for months!" Shock was evident on Sydney's face as she stared in confusion at the detectives.

"He also mentioned his belief that your baby wasn't his." Detective Daniels leveled his cool gaze directly at her. The statement pierced her heart and she was suddenly flustered.

"What? That's… that's impossible. He knew it was his. I was a virgin until him. He knew that." Her voice wavered, no longer coolly detached. "Why would he lie?"

"Were you in the habit of getting drunk at parties, Ms. Ross?" Detective Wills stared at her with flat brown eyes. They were very unlike Stephen's warm milk chocolate orbs.

"Of course not. You know who my parents are. Having a teenage daughter busted for underage drinking wouldn't help my father's re-election."

"Did getting pregnant?" Detective Daniels' raised his eyebrow at her again, aggravating her with his aloof judgment.

"Don't judge me. You don't know me at all. I don't get drunk. Ever. The only alcohol I've ever had was a glass of champagne or two at my parents' parties."

"Your parents supplied their underage daughter with champagne?" He looked at her doubtfully, clearly having swallowed her father's campaign rhetoric. Wholesome Family Values. What a joke.

"You have no idea what goes on at high-class parties of the powerful, Detective. At least I wasn't in the bathroom doing blow with some of the Congressmen in attendance."

Her voice was cool and unflustered again, every inch the socialite that she used to be.

"Touché, Ms. Ross. My apologies. And I'm not judging you. I'm just trying to get some answers. Your ex-boyfriend is claiming that he wasn't your boyfriend at all, simply a one-night stand. Who am I supposed to believe?"

"Well, since I was the one who was plowed down in a convenience store parking lot, you should realize that I have more of a vested interest in whether or not you find out who tried to kill me. Trust me, I will always tell you the truth. I have no reason not to. I have nothing to hide."

They stared each other down, silently daring the other to blink. She realized that he wasn't going to back down so she chose to speak again.

"My question, detective, is why are you spending your time focusing on my pregnancy? Does it really matter if my baby's father denies that it was his?"

"I believe it does," he answered, surprising her with his frank tone. "I think it's tied together. Would it surprise you if I told you that your parents don't want this investigation to continue? That they would be satisfied to just let the guy who hurt you walk? I just spoke with your mother this morning."

Again his face was impassive, but she felt sure that the question was orchestrated. He wanted to see her reaction. Again.

She didn't give him one, but she cringed on the inside. It was a devastating blow to realize over and over that nothing was more important to her own parents than their public appearance.

She knew the Why without asking. They didn't want public opinion of it, of her, to hurt the campaign. She was so tired of the endless freaking Campaign. It had been a part of her life since she was an infant. In fact, on more than one occasion, she had wondered if that was the reason she had been born at all…as a prop for the picture perfect, All-American family.

"No, it wouldn't surprise me," she sighed, trying to close off her expression so that they wouldn't see that it had upset her. As it was, she had a difficult time keeping her voice steady. "Was there anything else you needed from me?"

"I think that will be all for today. We just wanted to confirm the length of your relationship with Mr. Price. If we think of anything else, we'll let you know."

She followed them to the door, her eyes on the scuffed low pumps of Detective Wills as they walked. The woman's fashion sense hadn't improved. On their way out, the detectives passed Stephen as he strolled up the walk with a newspaper under his arm. They barely spared him a glance.

"Am I too late for the party?" Stephen asked lightly as he stepped into the house.

Sydney tried to smile but knew that the floodgates were about to open. She turned quickly, trying to escape to her room before the tears hit. She didn't want Stephen to witness it. She'd been so much better lately, much to his obvious relief. She didn't want him to start worrying again.

As she fled, Stephen stayed in place, staring after her in confusion. But it only took a second for the unmistakable sounds of her muffled sobs to reach him through her closed door and he quickly followed her.

He lingered in her doorway, watching her cry for as long as he could stand it before he strode quickly across the small room to sit on the edge of her bed, scooping her into his arms.

With Sydney's head on Stephen's chest and his arms wrapped tightly around her, she cried in wracking heaves until there was nothing left. When she finally raised her tear-streaked face to look at him, there were no more tears to cry.

"I'm sorry," she murmured quietly. "I actually felt better today, for awhile. But something they said about my parents was upsetting. I didn't mean to fall apart on you. I'm better now. I just needed to get it out."

"Don't apologize," he answered softly. "I wish I could give you good advice but your parents are a different species from mine. My experience doesn't apply to yours. But I promise you, everything will be okay."

Sydney listened to his heart beat for just a moment before she answered.

"I hope you're right. But sometimes, it just doesn't feel like it. The detectives told me today that my parents want the investigation stopped because it would hurt the campaign. They couldn't care less that someone tried to kill me. Do you know how that feels?"

He sighed heavily and tightened his arms around her.

"Syd, I don't know how that feels... I'm sorry. But if I could, I would take that pain for you. I don't want you to hurt."

"Trust me, I don't want to hurt, either. I'd gladly give it to you." She smiled ruefully.

"I can tell you this though, and I mean it. Whatever your parents feel or don't feel isn't a reflection on you. You're amazing. And if they honestly don't see that, then it is their loss. You're the best person I've ever met and you're going to have a great life. You don't need them to make you happy."

Sydney knew he was right. Her parents' feelings didn't define her but it was hard to convince her heart of that. She laid her head back on his hard chest, letting the scent of his masculinity surround her. The smell of aftershave and shaving cream floated lightly on top of the slightly musky fragrance of his skin.

She also realized that his chest wasn't the only thing that was hard. As she remained curled up in his lap, she felt the growing evidence of his desire for her and it set her on fire, regardless of the empty ache she felt inside.

She nudged against him, gently testing. Rejection was not something she could handle right now. Not after everything else.

He unconsciously pushed back against her and she felt his stiff rigidity resting against her. She wriggled closer, eliciting a sharp intake of breath from him. The sound of his need for her fueled her own, scorching through her as though someone had tossed lighter fluid on her and then lit a match. It came in waves, rippling and building. The air between them was so heavily charged that it almost sparked. She was suddenly breathlessly eager and flushed.

"Stephen, I want you," she whispered. "I can't help it. I've wanted you for so long. Please."

Heat flushed her cheeks and her skin practically tingled as she ran her hands against the solid expanse of his back. He groaned in response and buried his face into her hair.

"Syd, we can't. You're vulnerable right now and you don't know what you want-"

She interrupted him firmly. "I want *you*. Please, Stephen. You're the best person that I have ever met. I just want to feel close to you, as close as I can be."

She ran her hand through his hair and pulled his face down to hers. She knew the instant that he gave in. He tilted her back, softly cradling her, and lowered his lips to envelope hers.

She sucked him up hungrily, sliding her tongue softly between his lips as she ran her hands urgently over his body. She felt as though she couldn't get close enough to him, couldn't inhale enough of his scent, couldn't touch him enough. He appeared to share those thoughts as he pulled her as close as he could, pushing against her through her clothes.

Their breath was ragged as they experienced each moment, prolonging it and rushing it at the same time. He slid his hands over her soft body and buried his face into her neck, her scent sending him over the edge. He pulled her shirt over her head in one fluid motion. All traces of awkwardness were gone.

She unfastened her bra and he pulled it off for her, his eyes consuming her. He groaned again, crushing her to his chest.

She ripped his shirt off and savored the feel of their hot skin pressed together. Nothing on earth could compare to this feeling. The delicious, delicate teetering on the precipice of bliss. The charged anticipation, the sound of rasping breath, the silkiness of skin… Sydney thought she would explode.

Everything swirled together in her chest and she couldn't separate one emotion from another. Her desperate longing, the safety that she felt in his arms, the love that she felt in this room. The one thing that she could pinpoint was need. She needed him right now. And this was something that he could give to her.

Ten minutes of absolute perfection.

He arched against her, calling her name and then collapsed onto her. Rolling onto his side, he took her with him as though he didn't want them separated, even a fraction of an inch, a minute. They lay clutching each other, the experience taking on the feel of something almost spiritual.

He stared into her wet eyes. "I love you, Sydney."

"Well, now you tell me," she smiled, tracing circles on the slightly damp skin of his back with her fingers.

"You've known all along, haven't you?" he murmured, as he buried his face into the side of her neck. She felt him begin to react to her again and she responded by pressing herself even closer.

She shook her head. "I've been wanting you to see me this way for months."

"I've seen you this way the whole time." His voice was husky as he pulled her on top of him and began everything again.

Thirty minutes later, Sydney lay draped across Stephen's body, sweaty and spent. She was mulling words over in her head, trying to think of ways to vocalize her feelings about what had just happened but found herself coming up short.

She inhaled the heady scent of sex that lingered in the air like velvet and lightly trailed her fingers up and down his chest. Goosebumps formed where her fingers had been and she lowered her head to kiss them.

"I love you, too," she whispered, liking the substantial way the words felt in her mouth. Liking the way they felt as she applied them to Stephen.

She meant them this time. She had only thought she meant them when she had uttered them to Christian in the cramped backseat of his Porsche. Now she understood why people said to 'wait until you find someone special.' This experience had been so much more than she had ever dreamed that it could be. And she understood now why it was called Making Love. That's exactly what they had done. There was love here. The room was thick with it.

"I think we're probably going to hell now," Stephen murmured, even as he kept her clutched against him. "And it was probably illegal in 36 states," he added grimly.

"Why?" Her brow was wrinkled as she pondered his statement. "You mean because we're *distant* cousins? Or because of my age?" She snuggled closer, apparently unconcerned with either issue.

"Well, you're 18 now and I'm 24. That makes me a dirty old man, but it's not illegal. But the cousin thing..."

"Oh, please!" she rolled her eyes dismissively. "We're distant cousins, not first cousins and we didn't even know each other until last year! We don't even know how we're related so that's not exactly close familial ties! Besides..." She paused to kiss the sensitive skin by his nipple, "A lot of famous people have been with cousins- even first cousins! We're not unique."

"Hmm. Comparing us to Edgar Allen Poe doesn't ease my conscience," Stephen said wryly but sucked in his breath in spite of himself as she made a circle with her tongue.

"I wasn't thinking of him but now that you brought it up, he did marry his 13-year old first cousin. That's a lot worse than us!" Sydney smiled in the dying light from the window, her slender body still wrapped around his.

"I was thinking more along the lines of FDR. He and Eleanor were cousins of some sort.   Thomas Jefferson, Albert Einstein. They were both brilliant people who married cousins.   And those are just the ones that I remember from History class.   There's probably a ton more."

"Again, Thomas Jefferson isn't exactly who I would like to measure myself against. He might have been brilliant but he also fathered children with his slave women. And those guys were geniuses from previous centuries.   How about someone from the current one?" Even as he spoke, he couldn't help but smile at her efforts.

"Um." She paused while she thought, hovering above him. "Ha! Rudy Giuliani! He married his second cousin and he was the mayor of New York!" She smiled triumphantly.

"Yes, sweetheart. I know who he is."

Stephen's endearment stopped her moving fingers in their tracks, swelling her heart until it felt twice the size of normal.

Her parents were not big on endearments. Her dad used to call her Princess but she wouldn't exactly call it an endearment. She always felt that it was a reminder to himself that he was able to treat his daughter like a princess. It made him feel good. No one in her entire life had called her Sweetheart. It felt nice. Normal.

"And there are probably more but I don't care." She resumed her train of thought and continued the trail that her fingers were making on his body. "I don't care what anyone else does or thinks. I love you and you love me. I have never felt better than I do at this moment. That's all that matters."

"Is it?" He stared at her thoughtfully, studying the determined expression on her lovely face.

"Being together won't always be easy and not because of the cousin thing. You're right on that one. We're so distantly related that we're practically not related at all. Our parents are the only ones who will even know. I'm talking about the fact that we're from completely different worlds."

"Has that mattered so far?" She raised an eyebrow.

He had to admit that it hadn't. She had never complained once about not having something like steaks, air-conditioning or expensive shoes. She had worn her five dollar flip-flops just as though they were Manolo Blahniks. He was pretty sure that her old bedroom had been as big as his entire house but she had handled her change of circumstances with grace and character. It was one of the first things that he had noticed about her. It had been a pleasant surprise.

"No, it hasn't. I just wanted to bring it up. I can't give you the things that your parents could."

She stared at him incredulously.

"Things like what? Conditional approval? A broken heart? A lifetime of therapy bills? The things that you give me are much more important than an expensive car or a climate controlled closet. I have learned things from you... things like feeling safe and being loved no matter what. Those things are priceless. I'll never be able to repay you."

He stared at her in utter astonishment.

"Did you really have a climate controlled closet? What on earth for?"

She started to laugh, but her phone interrupted her train of thought. It rattled noisily on top of her bed-stand as it vibrated to signal a new text message. She looked at it in surprise. No one contacted her on it anymore except for Stephen.

Reaching over, she grabbed it and flicked it open. Her dad's name was on the screen in big, bold letters. Her heart stopped in her chest. She pushed 'Read' and then her breathing stopped, as well.

Paul, I'm horny. I want to see u. Jillian's gone until 10.

Her startled eyes met Stephen's as she turned the screen around for him to read. He read it quickly, surprise forming quickly on his face.

"What the hell?" He stared at her in puzzlement.

"He must have sent this to me by mistake. Obviously, it was meant for someone else."

A man? Shock made her impervious to anything else at the moment. She didn't feel anger or hurt or even embarrassment. She just sat in stunned amazement trying to soak it in. Her dad was having an affair. With a man.

An affair with a woman wouldn't have surprised her. He was flirtatious in a charming way with women of all ages. They usually liked it and he worked it to his advantage, flashing his bright white smile at them and making them feel special as the important senator gave them his undivided attention for just a second.

But a man? This was out of left field.

Sydney knew that he filed her contact info under "P" for Princess in his phone so she tried to think of a Paul that would have been filed next to her name. Someone that he meant to text instead of her. She drew a blank.

Until a vague memory started to form in her consciousness and a sick feeling lodged in her chest. It was blurry at first but sharpened as she thought about it with more focus. Paul Hayes was an Ohio senator.

Last year, she had gotten a screaming headache during one of her dad's fundraising parties. She had excused herself early and had gone upstairs to take some aspirin and go to bed. As she had walked down the long hallway to her bedroom, she heard low murmurs coming from down the hall. When she looked up, her father had been walking with Paul Hayes. They were murmuring quietly together and looked oh-so-surprised to see her.

At the time, she didn't think too much of it even though her father had clearly been startled when he saw her. She had just assumed that it was her sudden appearance that had surprised him. Now, she suddenly knew that it was the fact that she had seen him with Paul Hayes that had caused his distress.

Holy Mary Mother of God. Her dad was gay.

"Stephen," she began slowly. "I think my father is gay. He meant that text for Paul Hayes, a senator from Ohio."

Stephen didn't even ask her to explain how she had come to that conclusion. He just stared at her in stunned disbelief. His eyes were still slightly confused as he spoke, stating the obvious.

"Wow. Your dad's been lying to everyone."

She could tell from his tone that he was just as shocked as she was. Probably more so because he still had not been able to bring himself to believe that Randall Ross' campaign rhetoric was a lie. Family Values

First. What a crock of shit. She had seen him bald-faced lie to so many people over the years and do it with a smile. But this... this was huge. It could totally sink his career. And his marriage.

She wondered idly if she should tell her mother but she quickly abandoned that train of thought as a more pressing issue came to mind.

How in the world should she answer his text?

CHAPTER SIX

As she lugged the heavy bin of dirty plates, crumpled napkins and used flatware to the Sunshine Café's kitchen, Sydney realized something. She definitely didn't want to spend the rest of her life waitressing. And something else- she would never again under-tip a waitress.

She knew firsthand how hard it was and so did her poor feet. Who would have guessed that waitressing was so physically demanding? Her only consolation was that she was able to wear tennis shoes again.

She crossed the dingy restaurant floor, grinning ruefully at a regular patron as she went. She had been receiving all kinds of sympathetic smiles lately. Her regulars knew what had happened and pitied her.

She didn't like it. And they didn't even know the half of it. She sighed heavily.

They didn't know who she really was or about the lie that her family had been living, that not a single thing out of her father's mouth could be trusted because he couldn't even be honest about who he was.

Honestly, most of the patrons of the café didn't even know who her father even was because they weren't the type of people that followed politics. It was actually a blessing. It made it a little easier for her to get back to normal. Or her new normal, anyway.

It had been four days since she and Stephen had slept together for the first time. Four days since she had found out that her father was secretly gay. Four days since she had answered her father's text. *Sorry, you texted the wrong person.*

And four days of no response.

Every night, Stephen had held her until she fell asleep. Every night, he had whispered endearments and assurances to her, promising that everything would turn out alright. But she wasn't so sure anymore.

How could everything be alright when she couldn't trust a single thing? It was scary to realize that her whole life had been a lie while she never even had a clue. She couldn't even trust her own judgment.

What she did know was that her future was a blank canvas again. She could do anything she wanted to do and what she wanted was to get as far from here as possible. As far from her family and its lies as she could.

She idly wondered how Stephen would feel about moving to Indiana or maybe New York. She could go to college now. She had been accepted at Notre Dame as well as Columbia.

But she didn't want to move away unless Stephen would come with her. No matter what her future held, it was going to involve him, too. He was too important to her now. As she dumped her bin of dirty dishes, she made a mental note to discuss it with him that evening. She checked her watch. She only had 25 minutes left in this shift. Thank God. Her left heel had a blister and it was killing her.

As she re-entered the dining room, she pulled up the one bra strap that persistently slipped off the edge of her shoulder and then froze in mid-step.

At a tiny table in the back corner, away from everyone else in the small diner, a woman stood out like a sore thumb in an elegant cream-colored pantsuit and dark brown alligator Chanel shoes. She was looking out the window in agitation and drumming her perfectly manicured nails on the table. She was probably annoyed that she would have to be somewhere so… less than seemly. And that was putting it mildly.

Sydney was still frozen when Marge, the other waitress on duty, nudged her.

"Check out the snoot in the corner! Do you want to take her or do you want me to?"

Sydney swallowed hard. "I'll take her. She's my mother."

She could feel Marge's incredulous stare beating into her back as she doggedly trudged to her mother's table. She couldn't imagine what had made Jillian Ross venture into this neighborhood and into this diner to see her. Maybe the world was ending.

"Mom." Sydney stopped about a foot from the table and stared coldly at her mother.

"Sydney."

Her mother was every bit as cold. Disgusted with the place, agitated with her daughter, impatient with all of it. It was blatantly evident on her face.

"You need to come home."

"Why?" Shock was apparent in Sydney's voice even though she had intended to sound impassive. A plea to come home was not something she had expected or was prepared for.

"You know why!" Her mother snapped loud enough for an elderly couple at the next booth to swivel their heads in surprise. Her mother regained her composure and spoke again, with a quieter, more controlled tone.

"For your father. You cannot go on living here. Not in this neighborhood. Not with your cousin. Your pregnancy is over. You don't have to fight for it any longer."

Every word was an icy bullet aimed at Sydney's heart. Her mother only cared about appearances. Just like always.

"So, let me just recap. You don't really care that I am living in this run-down neighborhood. You don't care that I very recently lost my baby and the *only* person in the entire world that helped me or even cared was my *very distant* cousin, Stephen. You only care about what it looks like for my father's career. I just want to make sure I've got it right."

Her words were every bit as icy and she aimed them at her mother's head. Jillian Ross didn't even flinch.

"Sydney, stop being such an infant. You know how important this is. You've had your tantrum, now come home."

Her mother's face was hard. She was a beautiful woman but there was not even an ounce of warmth in her eyes. In Sydney's opinion, it detracted from her beauty.

"My tantrum? Mother, let me summarize for *you* this time. I don't give a goddamn about my father's career anymore. And you cannot make me come home. I turned 18 last week. I'm sure you meant to mail a birthday card, right?

"I will not be coming home. Not today, not next week, not ever. I already *am* home and I am finished being a prop for my father's campaign. Completely done. And don't think I don't know what this is *really* about. It's not about me. It's about my father and what I know."

Sydney spit the words, anger overtaking her so completely that she couldn't think straight. She didn't even care anymore if her mother hadn't known. She suddenly realized that she didn't feel any maternal connection with this woman. At all. All she felt was a strong dislike for her own mother. She should feel guilty but she didn't.

And she could see from the expression on Jillian's face that her mother knew exactly what she was talking about. When she spoke, it only confirmed Sydney's suspicion.

"You don't know anything." Icy tones, but her eyes betrayed her. There was fear there, hidden in the glittering pale blue depths.

"Oh, I do. My father is gay and he's been lying about it. But you already know that. How long have you known? Do you even care? Or is the only thing you care about the life that he gives you—the social standing, the money, the jet…"

She trailed off as she took in her mother's face.

"I'm right. You've known all along, haven't you? And you've tolerated it, hidden it in exchange for this life. You've given him a cover story and he's taken you with him up the ladder. Oh, wow. To think that I felt sorry for you for just a second when I found out. You're really pathetic. You should leave now. And don't come back."

Her mother stared at her for a moment, her mouth forming a hard, straight line as she watched her daughter speak. Color stained her cheeks. Sydney assumed it was from anger. It certainly wasn't from hurt or embarrassment. Her mother didn't care enough to experience those emotions.

"You'll be sorry, Sydney. Family is family. You can't count on anyone else. Your father can open all kinds of doors for you."

"I can open my own doors, thanks. And the only thing I'm sorry about is that we didn't have this conversation sooner."

Her hazel eyes shone like bronze as she stared her mother down, unflinching, unblinking.

Her mother held the stare for a minute longer and then gathered her purse and keys, stood to her full height and looked Sydney in the eye.

"If you don't walk out that door with me right now, don't bother coming back. Ever."

Sydney didn't move a muscle. She simply continued to hold her mother's icy gaze for a moment longer before she spoke. She was so still that she could feel her own heart beat.

"You're not really in a position to be giving me demands, now are you?"

Her mother shook her head derisively and stalked to the door, her heels clicking loudly as she went. She didn't look back as she climbed into her Jaguar and slammed the door.

Sydney felt her knees go weak and she slid into the nearest booth, breathing deeply. The exchange with her mother felt good in a strange sort of way, a sort of relief. But she also felt insanely sad that she didn't have normal parents or a normal life. This wasn't the way family was supposed to be.

Marge gripped her shoulder, appearing out of nowhere.

"Sydney, are you alright?"

Her rough voice was hesitant and as soft as Sydney had ever heard it. She looked up to find Marge's wrinkled face peering over her shoulder in concern. She felt a rush of warmth for this crusty old woman because she hardly ever showed her gentle side. In fact, Sydney hadn't even known that she had one. When she had first started, Marge had instantly disliked her. She had been afraid that Sydney would take all of the tips.

"I'm okay. Thanks," Sydney murmured and then smiled at her. Marge hugged her shoulders lightly and awkwardly. Sydney could easily tell that this type of situation made Marge uncomfortable and she was all the more grateful to her because of that.

"Family is hard, I know." Marge shrugged as though she was thinking of her own. "If you need anything, let me know."

She squeezed Sydney's hand and then tottered off, leaving a scented trail of aerosol hair spray and cigarettes behind her. Sydney gazed after her absently, replaying the scene with her mother in her head.

What had her mother really expected her to do? Move home and then what? It wouldn't make any difference. It wouldn't change anything. Unless... they thought that she might leak the information. The realization dawned on her abruptly.

They thought she was going to tell. Truthfully, the thought had never crossed her mind. She was pissed off at them but she didn't want to completely trash her parents' lives.

"Is this seat taken, Miss?"

She looked up to find Stephen standing over her. She had been so distracted that she didn't even notice the tinkling of the bells over the door when he walked in.

"Not any more. My mother just vacated it." She grinned wryly at him, trying to downplay the anxiety that still coursed through her veins.

"Seriously?" His chocolaty brown eyes searched her face for confirmation. "Are you alright?" He was instantly concerned and she felt warmth flood through her. The chatter of the diners around them faded out of her mind until all she could see was the handsome face in front of her.

"Seriously," she confirmed. "And my mother knew. About my dad, I mean. She's probably known all along. She's a piece of work. She told me that I had to come home and I told her no and she left. I think they think I'm going to tell someone."

"Are you?"

"No. I have no reason to do that. Maybe the American public deserves to know the truth about him, but they won't hear it from me." She absently played with the clean flatware laying on the table in front of her.

"You're a good person, Sydney Ross." Stephen reached across the table and grasped her small hand. "Want to go out for dinner tonight? Somewhere other than here?"

He glanced around as he spoke, taking in the cracked vinyl booth seats and the crooked owl clock on the wall. The owl's googly eyes were facing in two separate directions, its yellow beak faded.

"Where did you have in mind? I have about $20 bucks so far in tips."

"That won't be a problem. I sold my novel today and I'm getting an advance!"

Stephen's grin lit up his face and she sucked in her breath. He was incredibly handsome and she had not gotten used to it. She doubted that she ever could. She jumped up and flew into his arms, hugging him tightly against her.

"Congratulations! I knew you would do it!"

She inhaled him as he cradled her within his arms- too tightly for a public place, but for once she didn't care. It was hard to let go of old habits even when there was no need to constantly be aware of public opinion anymore.

It was a wonderful feeling. She briefly considered streaking down the street just because she could but decided against it. That might be going overboard.

"So, my lady," Stephen said, stepping backward and bowing dramatically low. "Where would you like to go? Your chariot awaits." She glanced out in the parking lot and saw his T-bird parked right out front.

"Hmm. You're the novelist. Aren't you supposed to have a good imagination? You choose!" She kissed him on the cheek, then turned. "I've got to clock out. I'll be right back."

He watched her walk through the swinging doors into the kitchen and it wasn't a second later before Marge rushed over to him, speaking hurriedly and glancing over her shoulder, presumably to watch for Sydney.

"Stephen, I don't know what is going on but it isn't good. Someone keeps calling here, asking for Sydney and then when we go to get her, they hang up. It's like they don't really want to talk to her, they just want to know if she's here. I haven't told her because that little girl's got enough to worry about. But someone should know. It doesn't feel right."

"You haven't told her?" He watched her wrinkled face as she shook her head.

"It hasn't really started bothering me until the past couple of days. The first few times it happened, I didn't think too much about it."

"How many times has it happened?"

"At least a dozen over the past couple of weeks."

"When was the last time?"

"Today. Maybe an hour ago."

"Do you know the voice?"

"No. It's a man- sounds like he is middle-aged. Definitely not a boy."

Stephen watched Sydney push through the kitchen doors again and smiled back at her gently when she grinned at him from across the room. He could tell from her face that she was tired. As much as she would like to deny it, she was still recovering from the accident.

"Thank you for telling me, Marge. Let's not tell her, okay? You're right. She has enough to worry about." He smiled at her and she smiled back, patting him on the shoulder.

"You're a good boy, Stephen. She's right to stick with you."

"Well, I'm glad you approve, Marge."

She walked away, her gnarled fingers darting out to snag the tip that someone had left her as she passed. She was secretly certain that the bus boys stole part of her tips. She tried not to leave them on the table too long in order to prevent the theft. Her eyes narrowed suspiciously as she saw one of them cleaning off a nearby table and she rushed over to grab that tip, as well.

"Hey, you come here often?" Sydney sidled up beside Stephen, bending to kiss his forehead. He tilted his head back to look at her, noting the slight flush in her cheeks.

"Oh, every once in a while. See there's this girl..." His voice trailed off as he grabbed her hand and kissed it.

"Really? What's she like?"

She squeezed his fingers as she spoke. She found herself wishing that they were in private. She'd suck on his fingers to see what effect it had on him. She was pretty sure she knew. She should be ashamed of herself, but she wasn't. Letting go of her inhibitions was starting to grow on her. Stephen appraised her before he answered.

"Well, she's young. And pretty. And a little bit sassy. Have you seen anyone around here that fits that description?"

"Not lately. But I'll let you know if I come across her. In the meantime, want to hang out with me?" She beamed her biggest smile at him and he almost collapsed. She was absolutely beautiful.

"Okay. I'll settle for you. For now. Just until I find the other one."

She punched him on the arm and then grabbed it, leaning into him in a familiar way that he loved while they walked out to his car. He opened her door like the perfect gentleman that his mama had taught him to be. As he waited for her to situate herself, he gazed absentmindedly at the trees rustling in the breeze and the cars lining the street.

His breath caught in his throat. Down the street, maybe two blocks away, a battered old black Trans Am was parallel parked. He could see a shadowy figure sitting inside behind the steering wheel. He couldn't make out who it was and he couldn't for the life of him imagine who would have enough balls to show up again in the same exact car that they had run Sydney down with.

He was careful not to act like anything was wrong and walked casually around to his side of the car, slamming the door as he got in. As he started the car, he asked, "Do you have Detective Daniels' card in your purse?"

Sydney looked at him in surprise. "Yes, I think so. Why?"

"Pull it out and call him."

She didn't ask any more questions because the look on his face was startling. She simply dug through her purse, found the card and dialed the number.

"Is it ringing?" Stephen barely glanced at her, instead keeping his eyes on the road, flickering from time to time to the rear view mirror.

"Yes."   She was apprehensive. Something was wrong and she didn't know what. It was an uncomfortable feeling.

"Let me have it." He held his hand out and she placed her phone in his palm.

"This is Daniels." The detective's curt voice was loud enough that Sydney could hear it through the phone. She craned her ears to hear it better.

"Detective Daniels, this is Stephen James. I just picked Sydney up at the Sunshine Café on the corner of Sample and West. The Black Trans Am that hit her was waiting for us down the street and it is following us now."

Sydney gasped and started to turn around but Stephen grabbed her arm and shook his head. She slumped against the seat and looked straight ahead, deciding instead to focus on not hyperventilating. She suddenly found it incredibly hard to breathe. She focused on long pulls in, then exhaling slowly, feeling her breath rush over her teeth. When the first breath didn't calm her, she tried it again.

"Yes, I can do that. It's only five minutes from here. Yes, I understand." Stephen flipped the phone closed and laid it gently back in her lap. It was apparent to her that he was being calm for her sake.

"Sydney, don't think about it. Everything's fine. You're with me." He grasped her hand for a moment, before returning both hands to the wheel. She saw him glance quickly into his rearview mirror again.

"Is it still back there?"

"Yes. We're going to lead him to a little park nearby. Detective Daniels is going to be there. Lucky for us, he was already in the area." He turned left and Sydney stared into her side mirror. Sure enough, she caught a glimpse of the black car just a few cars behind them. She sucked in her breath.

"Stephen, he's passing!"

The black car was weaving through traffic in order to get closer. Apparently, the driver wasn't so concerned with being covert anymore.

"Shit. He must know that we saw him!"

Stephen pressed the accelerator and the T-Bird edged forward, the heavy mass of the vintage car trembling as it sped up. The

Trans Am was right behind them now, directly on their tail.

"We're two minutes away. I need to keep him with us."

"I don't think that will be a problem."

Sydney's eyes were glued to her mirror, where she could plainly see the dented grill of the Trans Am hugging the back end of their car. She had given the car that dent. She swallowed hard.

"Can you see who it is?"

"No." Her face was panicked as she tried to look behind her. Stephen kept his eyes on the road, as he maneuvered the car through traffic, trying to make sure that they didn't lose the car behind them. Suddenly, their car lurched forward as the Trans Am slammed into their trunk.

"Oh my God—he's hitting us! On purpose!"

Sydney gripped the armrest so hard that her fingers turned white. They were rammed again from behind, so hard that Sydney's neck snapped forward like a rag doll and her teeth slammed together. Her arm flung out and braced the weight of her body against the door as she tried to anticipate the force of the next impact.

Stephen slung the T-Bird around the last corner and skidded to a stop in the dusty parking lot of the tiny neighborhood park. In a navy blue Crown Vic, Detective Daniels sat waiting. As soon as the Trans Am squealed by, he pulled out and flew after it in pursuit, red and blue lights flashing.

Sydney and Stephen stared at each other in shock. He reached over and pulled her to him, letting her tremble against his chest. She felt like a baby but all she could do was shake.

"Why is this happening?"

Her voice was small, like a child's. Stephen had to remember that while this situation would be unnerving to anyone, it was especially terrifying to her. She had spent her life in a glass bubble, removed from the real world.

"I don't know. But we're going to find out. I promise you that." His voice was laced with steely resolve and he meant every word. He would find out, no matter what it took.

They sat still for the next fifteen minutes while Stephen held her gently against his chest, stroking her hair and murmuring soothingly to her. She eventually calmed down and her shaking subsided. She had just pulled away when Detective Daniels' car slid smoothly into the slot next to theirs. He was out of his car and standing next to them almost immediately.

"He lost me and I couldn't get a good look at him. Did you see him?" he asked brusquely, as he leaned in Stephen's window. He was dressed in jeans and a black polo shirt so he was evidently off duty.

"No," Stephen answered. "Neither of us could get a good enough look at his face. He was wearing dark clothes and a black ball cap pulled down low."

"Well, Sydney... are you ready to talk yet?" The detective stared at Sydney pointedly.

"Detective, I wish that I could. I have no idea why this is happening. There is no one that I know of that hates me enough to want me dead. I can't figure it out."

Her voice was helpless and small and every ounce of her vulnerability shone through in it. Stephen glanced at the detective. Surely even he could hear it.

"Alright. Can you guys step out of the car? Let's sit down at the table over there and go over some things."

He strode purposefully toward a rickety picnic table sitting on the edge of the playground. He didn't even look back to see if they were following him- he just assumed they would.

He was right. They climbed out of the car and trailed after him, each taking a seat at the table. Sydney looked around nervously.

"I know this is silly but I don't feel safe out in the open. What if he is waiting for me? Somewhere where he can see me."

"It's not silly." The detective leaned toward her. "It's not silly at all. It's very possible that he will follow you everywhere you go until he takes care of whatever it is that he is supposed to do. Is he supposed to scare you? Hurt you? Take you? Kill you? We need to figure this out."

She took a deep breath and swallowed hard.

"I don't know how to help you. I really, really don't." She focused on his black leather loafers rather than his face.

"Let's start by you trying to remember *anything* out of the ordinary that has been going on. Anything- even if you don't think it is related." He waited, his penetrating eyes not leaving her face for a moment. His manicured fingers tapped the dirty table as he waited.

Stephen stared at her for a second before he spoke. "Well, there are a couple of things. I don't know if they are related..."

"It doesn't matter. Tell me and let me decide." The detective shifted his gaze to Stephen.

"Sydney just found out that her father is gay. That he has been gay all of these years and has hidden it from everyone. Except his wife. Sydney's mother has known all along."

Detective Daniels' stared flatly at Sydney, studying her.

"How did you just now figure that out? I thought you weren't speaking?"

"We're not. I figured it out the other night. It dawned on me when I was thinking about something else. What? Aren't you going to die of shock now?" She smiled a humorless smile. "Family Values First and all that?"

"No. Nothing in that screwed up world surprises me anymore."

He pulled out a pack of cigarettes and drew one out, lighting it and then inhaling slowly, staring off into the distance.

"You know those things will kill you, right?" Sydney smiled a tiny smile.

"I think you're in more danger at the moment than I am. Let's focus on you, shall we?"

He actually smiled back at her, something she hadn't yet seen. He had a nice smile and she found herself wondering why he didn't use it more.

He turned to Stephen. "What was the other thing? You said there were a couple."

Stephen looked hesitantly at Sydney. Her brow wrinkled as she stared back in confusion.

"What other thing is there?" she asked.

"Another waitress at the Sunshine told me today that someone keeps calling and asking for Sydney, but always hangs up before they have a chance to bring Sydney to the phone. He doesn't want to talk to her- he just wants to find out if she is there. Marge told me that he sounds middle-aged or so."

Shock was evident on Sydney's face, but she didn't react. She simply sat still, her hands clasped tightly in her lap, her knuckles white again. Stephen glanced worriedly at her, before addressing the detective again.

"Sydney is telling you the truth. She doesn't know anything. What do you think is going on?"

"I think that Sydney *does* know something. Something career ending." The breath froze in Sydney's throat as she stared at the detective in shock.

"You think my father has something to do with this? But I'm not going to tell anyone what I know. I wouldn't do that. Do you really think that he is trying to hurt me?"

"It's the best I've got right now. I think it's a pretty clear motive, don't you?" He stared back at her, almost kindly. "Sydney, when people get to the level that your father is, their priorities tend to change. They don't behave like the rest of us. Life gets skewed for them."

His tone held notes of sentiment and regret in it and Sydney watched him curiously.

"You sound like you know from experience."

"Unfortunately, I do. My step-dad is a senator. Paul Hayes from Ohio."

CHAPTER seven

Sydney and Stephen both stared at him incredulously, each silently trying to figure out what to say. Sydney felt the headache that had been building in the base of her neck turn into a pulsing throb behind her left ear.

Finally, she cleared her throat, glanced at Stephen and then looked back at the Detective. At the very least, this made sense. His taste was much too expensive for a detective. He came from money.

"Um. Detective, I'm not absolutely positive, but I think... I mean, what I'm trying to say is that... I think your step-dad is the person that my dad is having an affair with."

He stared at her blankly, not reacting.

"What makes you say that?"

His sharp eyes were trained unflinchingly on her, waiting for an explanation. She restlessly fidgeted with her fingers while she replied.

"Months ago, I saw your dad and mine walking together upstairs during one of my dad's parties. They were alone and I can't explain it, but they seemed much too familiar. The look on your dad's face was so... intimate. And then, I got a text from my dad the other night. It was meant for someone else, asking to see them because my mom was gone. He stores my name right next to your dad's in his phone. Like I said, I can't explain it, but it is a very strong feeling that I have."

The detective took another long pull on his cigarette, exhaling the smoke slowly. As it drifted upward in a gray cloud, he steadily stared at Sydney through it.

"You don't have to explain. Trust me, I know hunches. And this actually makes sense. There have been things over the years that have made me question..." he trailed off as he stared pensively into the distance. "But this changes everything, you know."

"How so?" She felt flustered; still confused and a little dazed from being chased by the Trans Am. Because her thoughts were muddled, she couldn't fathom why this knowledge would change anything.

He stared at her again, his blue eyes piercing hers.

"Sydney, I'm even more convinced that this is a clear motive."

She inhaled sharply, shaking her head slowly from side to side. He couldn't be right. Her father might not love her the way she wanted him to, the way a normal father would, but surely he wouldn't want to hurt her. Yet, even as she thought it, the doubts were already setting in.

The most important thing to her father was, and always had been, his career. He had watched a hundred different political careers destroyed by scandal and in her heart, Sydney knew that he would go to great lengths to keep this particular scandal from ever seeing the light of day. Her heart turned into a lump of ice buried within her chest. It was a possibility. A real possibility that her dad was behind this. She felt numb as she limply turned to look at Stephen.

The look on his face was one of disbelief and she could tell that he was mulling over the exact same thing. He reached over and grasped her hand.

"Sydney… surely not. He wouldn't…" But his voice trailed off uncertainly. He didn't even know her father and he was well aware of that fact. He had no way of knowing what Randall Ross was and wasn't capable of. He straightened his shoulders and turned to the detective.

"So what now?"

"Now, I do some more investigating. You know, my job."

The detective's voice was sarcastic, but not in an unfriendly way. It felt more like the joking between friends. This new revelation seemed to have plunged through the ice that had been between them from the beginning.

"But what should Sydney do?" Stephen was persistent. The incident today only escalated his concern about Sydney's safety. Particularly if her father did turn out to be behind it. It meant that deep pockets were funding the whole thing. And deep pockets could accomplish a lot. A whole lot more than he could.

"You need to maintain a low profile. I'll have a patrol going past your house regularly and if you see anything- and I mean *anything*- out of the ordinary, call me right away. Sydney, if I were you, I wouldn't go anywhere alone. Stay with someone at all times, you'll be safer that way."

He stared at her seriously as he spoke, making sure that she listened. He reached over and grasped her wrist lightly.

"Sydney, don't underestimate this. Your life could very well depend on your caution."

She felt numb as she stared back at him first uncertainly and then with resignation. She knew he was right. Her life was in danger- that much was apparent. Until she knew for sure who was behind it, she had to treat it as though it could be anyone. And honestly, it could be.

She fervently wished that instead of all those piano and tennis lessons she had taken throughout her life, that she had taken some self-defense classes instead. What was she supposed to do with a tennis racquet now, hit an assailant with it?

Detective Daniels stood and stretched, then turned to them again.

"You know, here's something to think about. He's probably trying to keep you quiet. If you are pro-active and release this information to the press then it is possible that you will take yourself out of danger."

Sydney stared at him apprehensively. "I don't think I can do that. Not without knowing for sure that my father is behind it. That would be a really vicious thing to do."

Something that her mother would be capable of, but not Sydney.

The detective nodded thoughtfully.

"I understand. It was just a thought. I'm going to go back to the station for awhile. You have my cell number. If you need me, call. In the meantime, until you hear from me, lay pretty low. Sydney, don't do anything in a scheduled pattern. If you normally go somewhere, don't. Do it at a different time. Shake up your routine. Make it difficult for someone to follow you."

She nodded and he turned on his heel, taking two steps before he turned back.

"Sydney? We didn't get off on the right foot and I know that is my fault. I apologize. I'm so used to people from your circle being insincere and entitled. And you are not. I never should have assumed otherwise." His voice was quiet but firm.

Sydney was astounded but before she could even respond, he had spun back around and continued walking to his car with long, graceful strides. She could see his gaze spanning the horizon, looking for anything out of place with his trained detective's eye. She supposed that she should start doing that as well, always being on alert. The thought was depressing.

Stephen stood and offered his hand to her, which she gladly took. He pulled her to her feet and then to his chest.

"It's going to be okay, Syd. I won't let anyone hurt you."

She knew that he meant it and that he wouldn't let anyone hurt her if he could help it. But what worried her was that Stephen was a kind-hearted person. She was pretty sure that in order to anticipate the actions of a psycho, you would need to understand them. There was no way that Stephen could think like that. Of that she was certain.

"Thank you."

She didn't voice her concern, only brushed a kiss across his soft lips and then quickly walked through the shadowy darkness to the car. She was done with this day—it had almost done her in. Literally.

* * *

She still dreamed that she was a mother. For the first several weeks after losing the baby, she had dreamed that she was rocking her daughter in a snowy white rocking chair.

The dreams would change and sometimes she dreamed that she was cradling an infant swathed in pink clothing in her arms. The baby's tiny hands rested against her chest and she could practically smell the powdery, heavenly baby scent.

Other times, she was rocking a beautiful little girl with caramel colored hair, just like her own. She was reading to her, relishing every minute of the quality time with her daughter. And then she would wake up. Every time. And every time, she felt the horrible, devastating emptiness of her loss rushing back to her.

As bad as those dreams were to wake up from, at least they were pleasant while they lasted. She had a taste, however brief, of what it was like to hold her daughter. Her new dreams were different. She dreamed that a baby was crying somewhere and she couldn't find it. She inherently knew that it was hers but she couldn't find it no matter how fast she ran or how hard she looked.

Tonight, she had woken up with a start, her body sticky with sweat—both as a result of the heat and of the panic that she felt while she was dreaming. The dream was so real that she could still taste the fear in her mouth when she woke up. The fear that she wouldn't find her baby.

As she lay still so she wouldn't wake Stephen, she stared at the crackled popcorn ceiling, faced with the reality that her baby was lost to her. It wasn't a fear, it wasn't a dream… it was her truth.

She would never hold her daughter, never find her daughter because her parents had thrown her out like medical waste. Sydney didn't even have a grave to visit her at. Resentment formed in her mouth and she swallowed hard to get rid of it. Dwelling on it wasn't going to make it any better.

She swung her feet over the side of the bed and sat for a moment to collect herself. She was never going back to sleep right now. Her mind was too restless, too disturbed from all of the events that had been jammed into her life lately.

For the past week, she had been on virtual lock-down. Stephen hadn't let her leave the house since the mystery assailant had tried to run them down. She had fallen asleep tonight while trying to put a face to the unknown attacker which is probably what had triggered her nightmares. She needed to clear her mind.

She walked as quietly as she could over the creaking boards of the aging house to the kitchen to grab a glass of ice water. As she stood at the sink, she stared out the window for a moment.

The light in her neighbors' house was on and she could clearly see into their home. The little blonde boy ran quickly through her field of vision before disappearing through a doorway that was out of her line of sight.

Interesting. It was 2:00 a.m. What kind of parents allowed their ten-year old to stay up until 2:00 a.m.? The boy had still been fully dressed. Apparently, he wasn't even thinking about going to bed yet.

She briefly wondered if his parents were even home before she shook her head and turned to walk into the living room, but she quickly turned back. She had caught something out of the corner of her eye... something not right. She scanned the side yard of their little house. It was empty, just as it should be. But the hair on her arms was standing up and she felt a strange sense of unease. Something was wrong.

She padded lightly to the back door and peered through the glass, leaving the light off so that her silhouette wouldn't be illuminated to anyone outside. Nightfall had turned the back yard into a palette of blue, gray, violet and black, with the silvery light of the moon falling upon the trees and creating rustling shadows.

She couldn't see anything that wasn't supposed to be there. The rickety wooden back fence, the faded red BBQ, some of the neighbor kids' toys. Everything was perfectly normal.

Just as she was shaking her head, amused at her own ridiculousness, a hand sheathed in a black glove plunged through the window of the door. Her immediate and single thought was only of the extreme noise that the shattering glass made in the stillness of the night.

She sprung backward but not quickly enough. The hand snaked around the corner and flicked the lock. A figure dressed totally in black with his face obscured by a ski mask lunged inside, snatched her arm and had yanked her back outside before she could even scream. It was just that quick... as smooth as a machine. The intruder had clearly done this before. He knew what he was doing.

He now had her clenched to his chest, one hand over her mouth. He shoved her roughly forward, his hand bunched up in the back of her nightgown. He didn't let go- he kept his hand there, in the small of her back, grasping the thin cotton. All she could do was comply, her knees bending woodenly as she walked barefoot through the backyard.

It had happened so fast that she knew there was no way that Stephen would have time to help, if he had even heard the noise at all. She hadn't had time to even blink or breathe. Her heart began sinking and didn't stop until they reached a white utility van parked down the block.

The man yanked the back door open and threw her roughly inside. He bent over her, quickly wrapping duct tape around her wrists several times and then slapping a long piece over her mouth. The sides of it stuck in her hair and she felt sharp twinges of pain as her hair pulled against the tape. He slammed the back doors and she was alone for a brief second.

There was no way she was coming out of this intact. She knew that.

A mesh metal screen separated the driver's seat from the back of the van and she sat hunched over as far from it as she could. Thoughts of survival raced through her mind as the van started to move.

She could kick the windows out... but, no. That was what you were supposed to do if you were trapped in a trunk- kick out the tail-lights. That was of no help to her now because there was no way she could kick through the laminated safety windows.

Her mind sped through her options until she bleakly realized that she didn't have any. Not a one. Her hands were bound, her mouth was taped. The only thing she could do was wait until the van stopped and maybe she could kick the guy when he opened the doors again.

She didn't have to wait for long. Twenty seconds later the van abruptly came to a halt.

"What the *hell*?!"

It was the first time the man had spoken and he wasn't happy. His thick voice curled around the last word, emphasizing his impatience with something that Sydney couldn't see.

He threw his door open, jumped out and slammed the door behind him. Sydney could hear muffled voices- too muffled. In a normal vehicle, she would have been able to discern words. But she couldn't now which meant that this van must have sound proof walls and glass.

Her stomach sank. But before she could panic too much, the back doors were wrenched opened again, the large man's shape loomed menacingly over her while he tossed in another victim.

She quickly registered the familiar face of the little boy next door. Her heart sped up and her chest started heaving as she tried to breathe.

What the hell was a good way to put it. Why was this kid here? His face was pale and terrified as their assailant slapped tape on him as well and then closed the doors again. Five seconds later, they were flying down the street. Away from her house, away from the safety of Stephen.

She looked at the little boy again. He was staring at her with wide eyes, unable to say anything to her. But his expression spoke a million words. And there was no way she could reassure him because she was in the same situation.

She leaned her head back against the cold metal of the van. The sky flying past the small tinted back windows didn't reveal any kind of clue whatsoever about where they were going. Once they turned left at the end of her street, she lost her sense of direction. Not being able to see anything but sky was incredibly disorienting.

As they waited in the dark, she tried to imagine what Stephen was doing. Had he heard the noise? Had he realized that she had been taken? Or was he still asleep- thinking that she was safely lying right next to him? A lump formed in her throat as she thought of him and she fought hard to swallow it.

The ride seemed to take forever but at the same time, she didn't want it to end. She was pretty sure she knew what was going to happen next. Her life was going to end. She wondered if it would be painful. Would she be brave? She gulped hard. Any hint of moisture in her mouth had evaporated from fear.

The van slowed and she tried to see out the window. The boy across from her looked at her in desperation but there wasn't anything she could do. Didn't he see that? She was sure that due to his age, he was still under the impression that adults could fix anything. She was sorry that he had to learn this way that it wasn't always true.

She heard muffled footsteps outside the doors and then suddenly they opened. As their assailant leaned in to reach for her, she kicked out at him with all the strength she could muster. Her heel caught him squarely on the chin, spinning his head to the side from the impact. She looked at the boy, motioning for him to jump out and run but neither of them had the opportunity. The man yanked them both out, one in each hand, and pulled her up next to his face.

"If you ever try that again," he rasped, "I will kill the boy. Do you want that on your shoulders?"

She assumed it was a rhetorical question but he shook her hard.

"Do you?" he demanded.

She quickly shook her head no and he nodded in apparent satisfaction.

"Good then. We have an understanding. Behave yourself."

He turned his attention to the blonde boy.

"Bet you wish you hadn't tried to play the hero, huh?"

He yanked both of him along with him to a small white house. The house looked perfectly normal with the only thing of note about it being the fact that it was so small. And that it was apparently in the middle of nowhere.

Sydney looked around her as best she could and couldn't see any other signs of life. They were in the country somewhere. But she couldn't imagine where. There were only in the van for an hour at the most. An hour would have gotten them to Gary, but she didn't smell the sulfurous smell that surrounded that town. She had no clue where they were. And she guessed that was probably the intention.

He dragged both of them with him into the house which smelled like wet, old carpet. She could tell that it hadn't been opened in a while. The air was so stale that it lingered in her nose like moldy cheese. She briefly wondered if this little house was actually a holding cell for their kidnapper's victims. She was certain by now that he did this fairly often. He had the mark of a professional.

He pushed them through the door of a small bedroom. She knew it was a bedroom only because of the small bed in the middle of the farthest wall. The room was utterly devoid of anything else and the one window was boarded off and nailed shut.

The man shoved both of them roughly to their knees as he stood behind them. Sydney squeezed her eyes tightly together. This was it. He was going to shoot them both. She could feel it. She wished there was something that she could do, but there was nothing. She couldn't even fight for her own life. Having her hands restrained was completely debilitating.

Suddenly he yanked the tape off of her mouth, resulting in pain a thousand times worse than yanking off a band-aid. A good-sized chunk of her hair came out with the tape and her cheek was left stinging sharply. She spun around so that she could look at him again, just in time to see him raise his arm in the air above his head.

The blow to her head was shocking in its intensity, but it happened so quickly that she didn't even feel it. She simply fell limply forward onto the floor, lying in a crumpled little heap.

The man didn't waste a second, quickly cold-cocking the little boy, as well, and leaving both of them unconscious on the floor as he closed and locked the door behind him.

CHAPTER Eight

Stephen stirred. Even in his sleep, he knew that something was different. He snaked out his arm to draw Sydney back up against his body, but her side of the bed was cold and empty.

He opened his eyes quickly and sat up. Ever since Sydney had lost the baby, she hadn't gotten up in the night to use the bathroom. He guessed that she was pacing the house, unable to sleep. With all that had gone on lately, he couldn't blame her and instantly felt guilty for not hearing her get up. She needed his support now more than ever.

He didn't bother pulling pants on, but instead strode out to the living room in his underwear. He figured that if someone wanted to look in his windows at this time of night, they deserved what they saw.

Streetlights shone weakly in through the windows, both illuminating and emphasizing the emptiness surrounding him. He stood in the middle of the living room, staring around him at the empty chair, empty couch, empty desk. Everything was empty.

"Sydney?"

His voice sounded hollow in the quiet house. As he examined his surroundings, he decided it probably wouldn't echo so much if they had more furniture. He was abruptly aware of the sparseness of his home. He had never really noticed before; but truthfully, he had never cared. He was never one to need things just for the sake of having them.

Sydney didn't answer him, which was odd. The house was so small that normally he could hear a cricket breathing outside the bathroom window from the comfort of his bed. And that was only a slight exaggeration. If Sydney were here, she would have heard him.

"Sydney?" he called again, louder and more anxiously this time, rapidly moving through each room.

She wasn't in the bathroom, the living room or on the front porch. His heart was accelerating with each step that he took. Surely she wouldn't have gone out by herself at this time of night- not now. As he stepped quickly into the kitchen, his heart lodged in his throat and stayed there, frozen.

The window in the back door was shattered... the glittering shards of glass scattered on the linoleum floor in haphazard disarray, a blatant signal that something was horribly wrong. Nothing else was disturbed, but nothing else needed to be. It was clear what had happened.

He froze in place, trying to breathe...struggling to swallow. His gut tightened up within him as though he had been sucker-punched. The cool night breeze rustling in through the broken window drifted over his naked body and formed goose-bumps, bringing him back to reality quickly.

Sydney had been taken. He knew it without taking one more step.

He darted back through the house, quickly finding his pants on the floor in the bedroom. He dug through the pockets as quickly as he could, finding his cell phone. He pulled it out and dialed Detective

Daniel's cell phone number with shaking fingers. It was of little consequence to him that it was 3 a.m. He could literally taste the adrenalin in his mouth as he waited.

The detective's voice was surly as he answered the phone on the fourth ring.

"This had better be important," he growled into the phone. Stephen knew the detective probably didn't know or care who was calling.

"It is. Sydney's been taken."

Stephen didn't know how he managed to speak because it felt like his entire body was frozen, completely numb. But his words came out normally, as though he was making a casual phone call. As though the girl he loved hadn't just been kidnapped from his house while he slept peacefully and blissfully unaware. His fingers betrayed him though. They shook as they held the phone to his ear.

"I'll be right there."

The phone went dead and Stephen held it motionless for a moment before snapping it closed and laying it down beside him on the empty bed. The silence was deafening. He gazed out the window mindlessly, not feeling capable of coherent thought, aware only of the loss and guilt that was consuming him already. It was difficult to say which weighed more heavily on him.

Both things collided together in his mind and he groaned. He had promised Sydney that he wouldn't let anyone hurt her. He was all she had and he had failed miserably. She was gone and he was to blame. He dropped his head into his waiting hands.

* * *

A noise had wakened her. And her head was throbbing relentlessly.

Sydney slowly opened her eyes and it took a moment for her to remember where she was. She was lying on a musty carpeted floor curled up in a fetal position. She unfolded her stiff limbs as she looked around the room.

The darkness was startling. The only light came from under the door and the cracks around the boarded up window. Everything else was bare with only a stripped bed pushed against the back wall.

She sniffed at the air. It was still stale and smelled like mold. Everything looked the same as it had last night when she had been tossed in here like a stray dog. The memory flooded back to her and she shivered. It had been real. For a brief moment, she truly felt as though it had been a realistic nightmare.

"Sydney?"

Her gaze flickered around the room to find the small voice that whispered her name and she zeroed in on the little boy hunched over in the corner. Her little blonde neighbor.

His skinny arms were wrapped around his knobby little knees and he shivered in the heat. Sydney decided that he must be in shock. It had to be at least 90 degrees in the cramped room. The memory of watching his small body get bound, gagged and thrown in the van beside her turned her stomach. Whoever did this clearly didn't have a conscience and that made him dangerous.

"Are you okay?" she murmured softly. He nodded silently, but his eyes glistened with unshed tears. It tugged on her heartstrings that he was trying to be brave. "I'm sorry. I can't remember your name right now. Can you remind me?"

The longer she was awake, the more the back of her head throbbed from the blow she had received the night before. She ignored it along with the dizziness that resulted whenever she moved.

"It's Danny—after my dad, Daniel."

She could hear the pride resonating in his small voice, even through the tenor of fear.

"Danny, why are you here? Why did he take you?"

She scooted towards him so that they didn't have to speak loudly. She spoke in low, hushed tones. She had no idea if their captor was on the other side of the door, but there was no reason to chance it. She kept glancing at the crack under the door, trying to see shadows moving on the other side- any movement that would signal that someone was there. But so far there was nothing.

"I got up to get a drink and I saw someone sneaking around your house from our kitchen window. I tried to get my parents but they wouldn't wake up, so I came outside to get a better look so I could call the police. He saw me, though." Danny sounded guilty, as though he had done something wrong so Sydney was quick to reassure him.

"Danny, you tried to be a hero. Thank you. Most people wouldn't have bothered.

But I wish you wouldn't have. Then you would be safely in your own house, instead of here with me." He shrugged his bony shoulders at her words.

"It doesn't matter."

"Yes, it does," she insisted. "But we've got to figure out a way to get out of here. Have you heard him outside of the door?"

Danny shook his head. "Nope. I think we're in the country somewhere. And there's a knocking sound on the wall every once in awhile."

That surprised her. It hadn't occurred to her that someone else might be here.

"Can you show me where?"

Danny got up and walked across the room, knocking lightly on a spot on the wall. Two seconds later an echoing knock resounded through their little room.

Sydney jumped up, ignoring the overwhelming dizziness that threatened to overtake her and ran directly to the spot. She put her ear against the wall and knocked again. Another knock in response. Someone was definitely there.

"Hello?" she called as softly as she could yet still loudly enough to be heard in the next room.

"Thank God, Oh my God. Please, can you help me?" A frantic female voice answered, as pounding commenced from the other side of the wall.

Sydney jumped as the pounding resonated in her ear and enhanced the pain in her head. Then she leaned close to the wall again.

"Please stop, he might hear you. We're in here but we can't help you. We're locked in, too. How long have you been here?"

The pounding ceased and Sydney breathed a sigh of relief. She instinctively knew that they should try and draw their captor's attention as little as possible. The girl didn't answer her so she tried again.

"My name is Sydney. What's yours?"

The only response was a desolate cry that creshendoed into a wail. Sydney beat her fists against the wall to try to get the girl's attention.

"Please calm down. Let's not draw his attention, okay? Calm down. It's alright."

There was sudden silence and then the girl hissed, "Are you crazy? Nothing is alright. Not anymore. You'll see."

She began crying again, this time more softly, but Sydney could plainly hear it through the wall. She turned to Danny and looked at him helplessly.

"You and I have to hold it together, okay? We can't figure out a way to get out if we aren't thinking clearly."

He nodded wordlessly and visibly began examining the room for anything that could be of use to them. His search was short-lived. There was nothing.

They were alone with four walls and a bed. There was absolutely nothing that they could use to escape. The boards were so tightly screwed into the wall that there was no getting them off with their bare hands. Danny's gaze locked with hers again. Both of their faces reflected what they each knew. They were helpless.

Chapter Nine

The days ran together in the tiny, isolated room. Time became an abstract concept. It was there, but they couldn't fully grasp it. There was nothing to mark it by.

Sydney tried to come up with games to play to keep Danny's mind off of their current situation but the entire time she was playing, she kept one section of her brain moving to try and hatch an escape plan. Time after time, she came up empty.

On her more hopeless days, she allowed herself to acknowledge that there was no way out of the room. The only thing she had left was to think of some way to outsmart their captor. If he ever returned.

Time and time again, she tried to talk to the girl in the next room but there was never a response. Every once in a while, they would hear low moans and crying so they knew she was still there. And still breathing. Her guttural howling attested to that. Sydney couldn't help but wonder how long she had been in there. The girl was clearly emotionally broken.

She and Danny huddled together on the sparse bed to sleep and she lost track of how many night falls had come and gone. Five, eight, maybe ten.

She only knew when it was night time because the tiny crack under the window went black and the room became entirely shrouded in darkness, an abyss so black that she couldn't see her hand in front of her face. As if it could get any worse, they had no water and no food. Sydney knew that at this rate they would be completely dehydrated soon and would die that way.

For the first few days, they had used the bathroom in the corner, their bodily waste creating an acrid odor in the room. It was humiliating and degrading but they had no other option. Since they didn't even have a bucket to use, she was pretty sure it had been planned that way.

It distressed her now that neither of them had used it for at least a day. She knew that it was a bad sign and tried to remember what dying by dehydration was like from what she had learned in Science. Did a person just go to sleep? No, that was hypothermia. She just couldn't remember. But then, her mind was slowing down as her body dried out.

She would kill for a drink. Of anything... water, coke, milk, juice. The memory of a slushie from 7-11 caused her to squeeze her dry eyes painfully shut. What she wouldn't give for just one single sip. Just one. It was incredible how she used to take such an important thing for granted. A one dollar slushie could literally keep her alive right now. Her life for a dollar. She shook her head at the irony.

Little Danny was getting weaker by the minute. He was smaller than she was, so dehydration was going to claim him first. She felt strangely maternal toward him and gathered him into her lap, stroking his hair back from his forehead and offering him empty assurances. She knew she was lying even as she spoke, but she couldn't help it. This was so unfair.

He lay limply draped over her legs, his small body trembling from time to time. She had never realized how quickly someone lost their strength without fluids. But why

would she? She had never been so deprived
of anything. From time to time, Danny
curled up into a ball, crying as his legs
cramped. She had also never known that
cramps were a side effect of dehydration.

"It's okay, Danny. It's alright. There,
see? It's gone."

She massaged his calf and he relaxed
again. He was pale, even paler than normal,
and his lips were cracked. They had been
bleeding but even the blood had dried up
now, forming a cakey mess around his
mouth. Hers were cracked too and she ran
her dry tongue over them. Of course she
found no relief. The arid coating of her
tongue snagged on the deep crack in her lip.
She had never been so parched. The dryness
of her mouth seemed to make the room feel
even hotter. It was a sauna now.

As she mentally tried to overcome the
misery she was feeling, a new sound
encroached on the periphery of her
consciousness. Tires crunching gravel and
the slight metallic squeak of brakes. A car
was pulling up to the house. Someone was
there. She yanked her head up in alarm.

"Danny? Wake up. You've got to wake
up, okay? Someone is here. It's probably
him."

She shook him lightly and he opened his eyes groggily. He was no longer fully cognizant and he struggled to focus. He stared in confusion at the blank wall.

"Danny? Can you hear me?"

He nodded his head and tried to sit up. Dizziness caused him to sway and he leaned into Sydney as he tried again. Her brain felt like mush and she couldn't think very well but she decided to drag him behind the door so that when it opened, he would be protected even if only for a minute.

She wasn't sure what her plan was yet, but she wanted Danny out of the way. She leaned him carefully against the wall and crept back to where she had been, directly in front of where the door would open. Dizziness caused the room to spin and she closed her eyes.

She heard footsteps falling outside of her door. Then another door opened and clicked closed. Muffled voices came from the room next to them and then terrified screaming and a thumping noise.

The screams went on and on and Sydney clapped her hands over her ears to block them out. Her heart pounded as she tried not to think of what was going on in there. She couldn't help but realize that she had heard a similar sound before through the thin walls of a hotel room. The thumping had a rhythmic, regular pattern. It was a bed lurching against the wall.

The screaming finally wound down into sobbing and the door creaked open again and latched closed with finality. The footsteps resumed and stopped just outside of her own door.

She took a deep breath in an attempt to calm herself and waited nervously. The door handle jiggled lightly and then opened, bringing with it a mild gust of fresh air and tinged with the pungent, musky odor of sex.

Light flooded the room and Sydney squinted her eyes against it. She couldn't see a thing. Her eyes had grown accustomed to the darkness over the past few days. As she struggled to see, the man spoke. This was a different man than had abducted her and his familiar voice chilled her to the bone.

"Hmm. I see you're still alive. Impressive. Did the boy die?"

Detective Daniels filled the doorway.

Sydney's eyes were getting used to the light and she could make out his shape and then his face. He had a cold smile on his handsome face as he stared at her with callous indifference. His voice was eerily empty of sentiment as he asked about Danny.

"Why have you done this?" she whispered in shock.

Her throat was so raspy that it took extreme effort to speak. She watched him with dry eyes, waiting for an answer. She had trusted this man. He was a police officer. Suddenly, what little hope she had left spiraled down to puddle around her feet. She found it morbidly ironic that in this moment, the worst moment of her life, her eyes were too dry to cry.

"Why do you think?"

His voice was still icy, but now it was taunting, as well. He took one step inside the room, wrinkling his nose in distaste as he did so.

His expensive clothing was in perfect order. His shirt was tucked in, his tie straight. Even though he had just raped the girl in the next room. Every cell in Sydney's body screamed at her to run but there was nowhere to go. Panic rose in her chest and she fought hard to control it.

"You made me think it was my father."

The dryness of her throat cut her off and she coughed. It felt as though her tongue was permanently stuck to the floor of her mouth, as though a puff of dust would come out when she exhaled. The thought made her cough again and the detective laughed.

"Of course I did. Why wouldn't I?"

"What do you want from me?" her voice was panicked, as he appraised her with cold eyes. "Are you going to rape me, too?"

She couldn't contain her disgust for him and his face hardened again.

"No. I don't want to rape you. What fun would that be? I know you won't beg. Yet. Maybe later, kitten."

Chills ran down Sydney's spine and she froze in apprehension as he took a step. He grinned maliciously, amused at her poorly concealed terror. He then walked further into the room and dropped a water bottle into her lap, his eyes locked with hers at every movement.

He watched in amusement as she greedily tore the top off and began guzzling, streams of liquid running down her chin. Tepid water had never tasted so good. She kept her eyes trained on him as she drank but lowered the bottle when she remembered little Danny. She started to scoot over to him but the detective stepped in front of her, halting her movement.

"No. That water is for you."

"Please. He's going to die. Soon." Her eyes beseeched the detective's hard face.

"Am I supposed to care?" His face was an emotionless mask as he spoke.

"Please. He's just a little boy."

"He's unimportant. But I need you alive."

"Detective. I'll do anything you want me to do, but please, *please* let me help him. He hasn't done anything to deserve to be here."

Her face was pleading as she begged. Her eyes kept flickering to Danny as she realized that she hadn't seen him move since she had placed him behind the door.

"And have you?"

Before Sydney could even respond, he continued.

"Why is this one little boy so important to you? He's nothing."

The detective walked over to Danny and gazed down at him for a moment, his lip curled in contempt. He nudged Danny's leg with the toe of one polished Italian loafer before he turned his gaze back to Sydney. "He's beyond help, anyway."

"No, he isn't!" Sydney insisted. "Please, just let me give him a drink."

"Stop begging. It's beneath you."

He jerked his head toward the boy in one curt gesture and Sydney immediately jumped up and ran to Danny. She knelt beside him, cradling his head in one arm as she gently held the water bottle to his mouth.

"Danny, drink it. Come on, be a good boy."

His eyelids fluttered and then opened. He looked at her and then weakly drank the water.

"That's right, that's good. Drink just a little more."

Her voice was soft and encouraging as he drank the life-sustaining liquid. The entire time, Harrison Daniels stared at them both in disgust.

"I'll never understand women."

His lip was curled and she could tell that he didn't *want* to understand women. She suddenly understood from his tone why he had been so cold to her from the very beginning.

He disliked women. He felt as though he was above trying to think like one. She knew it as surely as she was breathing but couldn't imagine what had happened to him to make him feel in such a way.

"You don't like women.   Why?" she questioned, staring up at him.

He stared at her coldly.

"It's cute that you think you are in a position to question me."

He turned his back on her for a moment, a brief second- the space of one breath. Then he turned back to her.

"Do you want to live?"   His smile glittered in the light.

"Of course. But I know you aren't going to allow that.   So why don't you just go ahead and kill me now? Why stretch it out? Do you need to make me suffer? You need to break me so that I will beg while you rape me?"

"Partly. But I need you to do something for me.   And then I might let you live. You're going to be a movie star. You'll like that, won't you?" His tone was mocking.

"What kind of movie star?"

"Any kind I want you to be.   But for now, I'm going to give you a script and you're going to memorize it. Then you are going to perform for me on camera- perfectly. Or he dies." He jerked his head toward Danny again. "But if you are good, I'll let him live."

Sydney eyed him carefully. She knew that there was no way in hell that he was going to let either of them live, not when they could both identify him. She chose her next words carefully.

"I promise to do what you ask if you will give Danny food and water. Will you do that?" She watched his reaction, trying to gauge his intent from his expression.

"That's a small enough price to pay. But what about yourself? Don't you want to eat?"

"Of course I do," she whispered, hating that she would admit it to him.

But she was so, so hungry. Her stomach felt as though it had collapsed upon itself. It had been overshadowed completely by her desperate thirst but now that she could think a little more clearly, her hunger pangs were almost overwhelming.

He smiled at her again, the perfectly polite smile of a host, before he ducked out the door and closed it behind him. He was only gone for a minute before he returned with a large box. He set it down in front of her.

"This is full of peanut butter sandwiches and chips. There are also bottles of water. Be careful because it has to last until I come back next time. Now, I'm going to take you to the bathroom and you are going to clean yourself up. And then we're going to make a movie."

Fear stilled her heart. She could only think of one kind of movie that a man like him would want to make with a woman. And since she had already ascertained that this particular man hated women, she couldn't even imagine what kind of horrible, degrading things he would make her do in his movie.

She took a deep, stilling breath before she nodded. The detective took a step toward the door, then turned to her again, his voice icy.

"One more thing. Don't try to run from me or I will kill the boy and it will be a violent, bloody death. Don't doubt it," he threatened.

She didn't. She could tell from the steely expression on his face that he wouldn't hesitate a millisecond before killing Danny. She turned to the frightened little boy.

"Don't be afraid, Danny. I'm going to go with this man to help him with something. While I'm gone, I want you to eat a sandwich and drink a bottle of water. Okay?"

Danny nodded but his expression was worried. Sydney turned and walked with detective Daniels out the door, waiting while he paused to lock it. She took note that it was padlocked into a hinge on the door. She wondered if she would be able to force it open. She silently vowed to try if he left them here alive.

The detective escorted her to a dingy bathroom which was a hundred times dirtier than Stephen's had ever been.

Sydney's thoughts wavered briefly at the thought of Stephen. She knew he was probably beside himself right now. She silently said a prayer for his protection and then turned on the water in the sink as Detective Daniels stood silently at her side. While the water ran into the grimy sink, he handed her a wash cloth and a hair brush.

"Clean up," he demanded.

She looked into the cloudy mirror and studied her reflection. She had sunken circles under her eyes which were probably a combined result of dehydration and lack of sleep. Her skin looked incredibly pale from being closed in the dark room. She was only a shadow of herself.

She wiped her face with the rag and then combed her hair. She tried not to notice that there was dried blood on the wall beside her. When she was finished, she turned to the detective.

"I don't suppose I can have a toothbrush?"

He shook his head impatiently. "No one is going to notice your teeth."

He grabbed her elbow and dragged her from the bathroom into another bedroom where there was a single chair set up in front of a camera. She was instantly confused. She expected to see a bed in front of the camera. Not this.

She turned to him in surprise. "What are you going to have me do?"

He thrust a paper into her hands. Her eyes skimmed over it and with every word she read, her heart sped up a little bit more until it felt as though it would leap from her throat. Her fingers shook as she held the paper and finally she looked back up at him.

"Why do you want me to expose my dad? You suggested this awhile back, too— that I leak this to the press. Why?"

"It's not your father who is important in this equation," he ground out through gritted teeth. He shoved her harshly into the chair and began adjusting the camera. "And if you had listened to me then, you wouldn't be here now."

Sydney tried not to think about that.

"Okay, fine. Why do you want to expose *your* father?"

She thought she had seen every kind of backstabbing in her previous life, but this was a new kind of betrayal. This betrayal stemmed from a deep-seeded hatred.

"He is *not* my father."

Detective Daniels practically spit the words at her and she cringed from the bitterness they contained.

"Now, you are going to look into the camera and say what was on the script. Word for word. This is your only chance of getting out of here alive so be convincing."

Sydney swallowed hard as the light on the camera turned red. It wasn't so much that she was adversely against reading the script but she was afraid of what would happen to her after she read it. Once it was finished, he would have no more use for her. But she had no choice, so she leveled her gaze at the blinking red light and began to speak in a strong voice.

"Hello. My name is Sydney Ross, daughter of Illinois senator Randall Ross. I am sending you this videotape as a public service announcement of my own because I need you to know something about the official that you continue to elect to office. It is important that you know this information before the upcoming elections.

"My father, whose slogan has always been Family Values First, has been lying to you and to the entire world. He has been hiding his sexual orientation as a homosexual for years... and his partner is none other than Ohio senator Paul Hayes."

Chapter Ten

Stephen anxiously paced through the house, his nerves frayed and willing his phone to ring. Ever since Sydney was taken, he had spoken with the detective several times daily. In fact, he had spoken with him so much that he now called him Harrison.

His first impression of the detective couldn't have been more off base. Throughout the entire hellish last week, while he waited to find out anything about Sydney's whereabouts, Harrison had been nothing but gracious and patient.

Stephen had to admit that he had practically hounded the poor guy, begging for any new tidbit or a lead of some sort. But Harrison had kindly answered the phone every time, attempting to calm Stephen's anxiety with the experience that he had developed over the years in similar situations.

Kidnappings, that is. But even Harrison had to admit that this situation was unique due to the important players involved. Which was why he had instituted the gag order for everyone involved. It was not going to be leaked to the press for any reason.

Something about that seemed wrong to Stephen. He wanted the whole world to know so that the whole world could be looking for Sydney But on the same token, he knew that if they tipped their hand to Randall Ross, the whole game could be over.

He seethed just thinking about Senator Ross. In fact, when one of the senator's campaign commercials had aired earlier that morning, he had thrown his glass at the television. Family Values First. What bullshit! If only he had listened to Sydney, really listened, when she tried to tell him.

A soft knock at the front door startled him from his thoughts and he quickly strode across the room to answer it. Detective Delores Wills stood in front of him, her face tired.

"Stephen? How are you doing?"

Her tone indicated that she was sincere. He imagined how he must look to her. He hadn't showered in a couple of days, his eyes must be blood shot from lack of sleep and he was jittery from too much caffeine. He probably looked like a strung-out druggie.

"Oh, not that great, I guess. I mean, if you want the honest answer." He swung the door wide and she entered, standing next to him rather than walking any further inside.

"I do. Stephen, you should get some sleep. If anything comes up, we'll call you. First thing. You have my word." Her tone was almost warm.

"I wish I could sleep, detective. I haven't been able to. Every time I close my eyes, I see her face and it reminds me that she isn't here. Do you think she's still alive?"

He swallowed hard as he stared at Detective Wills forcefully. He really needed her honest opinion right now.

She studied him for a moment before answering. "I don't know. We haven't gotten a ransom demand yet which seems to further point towards Sydney's father. Detective Daniels is working on attaining a court order from a judge to search the Senator's home."

"He wouldn't be stupid enough to keep Sydney in his house!" Stephen was exasperated. Were the police really so dumb?

"No, he probably wouldn't. But there could be clues in his house that might implicate him further."

Stephen relaxed again. He should have known that- at the very least from all of the crime scene television shows that he watched. His sleepless state was really messing with his cognition.

"I'm sorry, detective. I'm being rude. You came here for something. Can I help you?"

"Actually, I was just stopping by to check on you and to see if you had heard anything. Anything at all." She looked at him. "Because if the perpetrator contacts you, you need to let us know even if he says not to."

"I haven't heard a thing, detective."

His shoulders slumped as he realized that she really didn't have any news for him. He had been hopeful when he opened the door.

"But you have my word that if I hear *anything,* you will know about it." Detective Wills nodded before she stepped back out the door, turning in the doorframe.

"Stephen, really… get some sleep. You look terrible. There's nothing you can do for her in this capacity. We'll call you the minute we know anything. And here—take my card. It has my cell number on it in case you can't get a hold of Detective Daniels for some reason. Just in case you hear something."

She pressed her card into his hand and turned again, walking briskly down the sidewalk to her car, not looking back.

Stephen closed the door and leaned his head against it. She was probably right. He should get some sleep. He couldn't even think straight anymore. He felt like he was losing his mind. He slumped dejectedly into the bedroom, where he dropped onto the bed fully clothed. He laid his cell phone on the pillow beside him and closed his eyes.

* * *

It had been several days since Sydney had made the tape for Detective Daniels. After the taping was over, he had surprised her by yanking her back to the other bedroom and throwing her inside with Danny. She had expected that he would kill her but he didn't.

They had heard him rustling around in the house, then they heard the tires crunching on gravel again as he left. Then they had stared at each other. He had really left them there alive.

It was a surprising turn of events.

Sydney had wasted no time trying to break the door down. She knew that if she could just kick hard enough, the padlocked hinge on the other side would break loose. But so far, it hadn't. And she had been trying hard and often. Her poor feet had deep bruises to prove it.

They were down to their last peanut butter sandwich although they still had several bottles of water left. The stench of ammonia was almost unbearable in the room, like an overfilled stable or an overflowing sewer pipe. Sydney knew that if they ever got out of there alive, the smell would leave an indelible impression in her nose. She would never get it out.

She edged up to the wall and knocked on it again in an attempt to communicate with the other girl. So far, her attempts had been futile. The girl didn't want to talk. Today, however, she surprised them.

"What do you want?" Her voice was impatient, as though she had other things she needed to be doing.

"I want to know about you. Why are you here?" Sydney's voice was firm and slightly demanding. She couldn't imagine why the girl didn't want to communicate.

"Does it matter? It doesn't change anything."

The girl's voice was pitifully hopeless and desolate. Sydney's stomach sunk a notch lower just listening to it. Would that be her in a few months... a hollow shell of a person?

"It matters to me. Do you have a name?"

"Of course I do. It's Deidre."

"I like your name, Deidre. Why are you here? Do you know?"

"Of course I know. I know his secret."

"Whose secret? Detective Daniels?" Sydney's head snapped up in interest.

"Heaven help me... yes. Harrison's secret." The girl started sobbing again, pitifully mewling.

"Deidre, get a hold on yourself. What is his secret? And how do you know it?"

The sobbing melted into sniffling.

"I dated Harrison a couple of years ago. He got drunk one night and told me things—things that he didn't really want to share. The next morning, when he sobered up, he completely changed. He was like another person. He told me that he didn't want to have to do it, but that I was forcing him to because I tricked him into telling me things. And then he brought me here."

The crying started again. "But I didn't trick him. I didn't ask him to tell me anything!"

Sydney let her cry for a few minutes longer before she interrupted her again.

"So, he's held you here for the past couple of *years*? Hasn't anyone filed a missing persons report?"

"I don't have any family. I was an only child and my parents are dead."

The perfect scenario for a psychotic cop wanting to hold her captive. Sydney shuddered and chills ran down her spine.

"I'm so sorry, Deidre. But I do have family. And they're going to know that I'm gone and they'll try to find me."

She hoped. She knew Stephen would but she couldn't speak for her parents. Not after that video tape was released to news stations as per Harrison Daniels' plan. They would think it was her just desserts.

"Deidre, what is Harrison's secret?"

"His step-dad molested him for years. Ever since his mom married the guy back when Harrison was six." Horror slammed into Sydney's chest like a cement truck.

"And his mom never did anything to stop it even though she knew. She just looked the other way. He's so fucked up now that he doesn't know if he is coming or going. But he hides it really well. I never even knew it until that one night. He said it makes him do bad things. And he does. He does really bad things."

Deidre's voice wavered and then she collapsed into sobbing again. This time, Sydney let her be. She didn't try to get any more information from her. The girl had clearly been through enough.

No wonder the detective hated women. His own mother had knowingly left him at the mercy of a pedophile. And his step-father had preyed upon an innocent, vulnerable boy to get his rocks off. Her skin crawled at the thought and she felt like she was going to throw up. And she had thought that *her* life had been bad. This made her life look like the Andy Griffith show.

She felt a piercing sadness for the child that Harrison Daniels' had been. At some point, he had been a vulnerable little boy just like Danny. And years of being exposed to a monster had turned him into one. She tried to force all traces of pity from her heart because it wasn't going to help her. She couldn't change his past but she could try and change her own future.

She got to her feet again and started kicking at the door with all of the strength in her slight body. The door jarred with each blow as her foot connected with the old, dry wood, but it held firm. She doggedly continued kicking it with her aching feet. She grew increasingly frustrated until she slid down the wall and slumped to the floor. Who was she kidding? Had she really thought she could kick down a padlocked door?

As she sat with her elbows on her knees, staring dejectedly at the floor between her legs, a montage of images flooded her mind. Stephen's face as he kissed her for the first time, Stephen's eyes as they crinkled while he laughed. Stephen holding her hand for days at a time in the hospital.

His image morphed into the cruel form of Harrison Daniels. The detective smirked at her, taunted her, mocked her... until she felt a sudden rage fill her up and overtake her completely. She was not going to let that monster kill her. It wasn't going to happen. He had no right.

She wiped the frustrated wetness from her eyes and jumped up with renewed energy. The door took the brunt of her agitation as she leveled her best rendition of a round house kick at it.

It felt so good that she did it again. And again. The only other time she had used kicks like this was with her personal trainer, but they felt much more effective now as the sole of her foot connected solidly with the door.

When her thigh got tired, she switched to her other leg and then to front kicks... beating the crap out of the door tirelessly as her rage consumed her and fueled her with adrenaline.

To her surprise, the hinge gave a little as though one of the screws had come out. The door opened by a half inch. It only increased her aggression and she kicked all the harder, giving it everything she had left- every possible ounce of strength.

With every kick, the metal hinge creaked and rattled, giving her hope and pushing her on. With her final kick, the door gave way with a groan. It flew open and she heard the metal hinge drop to the ground.

She stared at it in shock for a second and then realized that Danny was staring at her with an expression of awe. She was sure that she must look unbelievable, as small as she was, kicking down a locked door barefoot.

She guessed what she had always heard was true. A person really could pick up a car if they were scared or desperate enough. She had just kicked down a door. That was pretty bad ass stuff. She hoped that she lived to brag about it.

"Come on, Danny!"

She grabbed him by the arm and dragged him with her as she rushed through the door. She stopped at the room next to theirs and examined the padlock. There was no way that she could kick it down from this side.

"Deidre? This is Sydney. I'm out here. I kicked down our door. You can do the same thing!"

"I can't, Sydney! I'm not strong enough!" Deidre started beating on the door with her fists, but the door didn't budge.

"Deidre, use your feet. Kick it!"

Sydney pushed Danny behind her as Deidre began kicking at the door. The door thudded with each impact, but stayed intact.

"I don't have any shoes. I can't kick hard enough! I haven't eaten in weeks. Go without me and bring back help. He could come back any minute- go!"

"Deidre, I really don't want to leave here without you. With us gone, he could move you."

Deidre interrupted her. "Just go! There's nothing else to do. But please, please Sydney. Please, bring back help! You don't know the things he does to me..."

Her voice trailed off, but the desperation it contained broke Sydney's heart and it was all she could do to turn away.

"I promise you, Deidre. I'll bring back help."

Sydney didn't waste even another minute as she tugged Danny along with her and she found the back door. As they stepped out into the light, the warmth from the sun washed over them and she felt free with a magnitude that she had never felt before. Absolute liberation.

She looked around. There was nothing around them but cloudless sky for what appeared to be miles. Fields, crops and an empty road. They were definitely in the country. They were standing on the gravel driveway a few feet away from a faded white propane tank.

So, they were far enough from town that the gas company didn't pipe natural gas out here. From the position of the sun, she guessed that it was late afternoon, so it was important to get moving. She didn't want to be stuck in the country at night.

She stopped for just a second to kneel on the sharp rocks beside Danny, her heart still thudding in her chest.

"Danny, we're going to have to walk a lot today. But we've got to get as far from here as we can. We've got to find some help for Deidre before he comes back. Okay?"

He nodded and put his hand in hers, tugging her to get started. She let him pull her down the sharp gravel of the driveway and she only looked back once. The tiny house seemed so sad, standing there alone, that she shuddered.

The fact that she was leaving Deidre in there, completely vulnerable, made her nauseous. But there was no help for it. She gripped Danny's hand and continued walking briskly in a direction that she hoped would lead to help.

Chapter Eleven

He couldn't take it anymore. Sydney had been gone for two weeks. The walls of his house were closing in on him and he had to get out for awhile. He didn't want to leave for long because if Syd were to come home, he wanted to be there.

Stephen paced the worn hardwood floors of his living room like a caged lion. His patience was frazzled to the point that it was no longer existent. Although the detectives had been kind to him, they still hadn't found Sydney. And it had been *two weeks*.

So much could happen in two weeks time. So many things that it terrified him just to think about them. His cell phone rang in his hands and he answered it on the first ring.

"Hello?" He answered hopefully.

"It's Daniels. We've got something interesting here. Someone mailed a videotape taken of Sydney."

"Is she alright?" Stephen asked anxiously.

"She appeared to be. But her message was interesting. She wants the world to know that her father is gay. She looked strong and healthy and it almost appeared as if she was videotaping herself. Do you think it is possible that Sydney ran away on her own accord so that she could get this tape out before her father could get to her? Maybe she was trying to protect you, for instance."

"No." Stephen's answer was immediate. "She wouldn't do that. She trusts me and she would've just told me. She wouldn't leave in the middle of the night and make it look like an abduction. She wouldn't do that to me." He felt confident of that fact.

"Maybe she thought you wouldn't let her go any other way. Maybe she was trying to keep you safe."

Stephen protested again. He knew she wouldn't have done that. She would want to keep him safe, yes... but she would know that his worry would be unbearable.

"It was just a thought," Harrison added. "I'm following up on the videotape to see if the post office it was mailed from has surveillance footage. We'll find out soon enough if it was Sydney herself or we'll get a description of whoever is holding her."

Stephen felt himself bristling. Clearly, Detective Daniels believed that Sydney was safe and sound somewhere, intent on ruining her father's life. Stephen knew her better than that, but how could he prove it?

"What are you going to do with the video?"

"We're holding onto it for a couple of days. Chances are, if it was sent to us, it was also sent to a news station. We'll see if it emerges anywhere else in the next couple of days and in the meantime, if there is surveillance tape at the post office, I will review it."

The detective had lost his air of urgency, Stephen could feel it. It filled his heart with dread. If the detective wasn't going to put all of his energy into finding Sydney, how in the world was Stephen going to find her?

* * *

After trudging a couple of miles, Sydney and Danny noticed a grain silo rising out of the horizon and they automatically began walking faster to reach it, even though Sydney was limping painfully.

Danny hadn't complained a single time even though he was only wearing rubber flip-flops. Sydney knew that he must have blisters. When they saw the silo, he took them off and began walking barefoot.

As soon as a cozy little farm house situated next to the grain silo came into view, they picked up the pace even more. Just having it in their sights lifted their spirits and made it easier to trudge down the empty road, hopefully to someone who could help them.

Ten minutes later, they cautiously approached the driveway. They crept silently up to it, attempting to observe any signs of life before approaching the house. Sydney was slightly nervous that whoever lived here might be on Harrison's payroll. It looked like a regular farmhouse but she couldn't be too careful.

Harrison was smart. And he had money. It would make sense to hire someone to live in the nearest house to his little hide-out. That way, if anyone did escape, they would run directly to someone on his payroll. Sydney shuddered thinking about it and concentrated on the farmhouse in front of her.

A barn was directly behind it right next to a pasture full of cattle. There was a grain silo bursting with corn and barn cats running rampantly around the property. If this wasn't a working farm, then they had done a really good job of imitating one. Sydney decided to chance it. She didn't know what other option they had. She couldn't see the next nearest house.

They rushed up the driveway just in time to meet a ruddy-faced farmer emerging from the barn. He was wearing overalls and a greasy cap and stared at them in surprise. Sydney couldn't quite blame him. She was wearing a nightgown and barefoot, while Danny looked terrified. They probably looked like refugees.

"Excuse me, sir?" She stepped closer, pulling Danny with her. "We have an emergency. Could you help us?"

She quickly filled the farmer in on their situation, including the fact that they had left a girl behind. The farmer's face grew more alarmed with every word she spoke.

"Miss, we need to call the police!" He wheeled around toward the house, but she grabbed his arm.

"Please, don't. He *is* the police." The farmer stared at her in horror.

"Miss, you've been through a lot. I think we should sit you down and I'll call the police for you. There is no one else to call."

Panic flooded her. She had not just escaped from a monster just to have this old farmer call him and lead him right back to her.

"Sir, please. I have been through a lot, but I am perfectly clear on this point. A detective has done this to us. If you call him, he will come right back out here and take us again. Please. Don't call the police."

The farmer studied her for a moment and finally nodded. He seemed to believe her.

"If we can't call the police, then how can I help?" he asked, his face confused.

"Do you think… I mean, could you… could you drive us back down there? And do you have something to break the lock?

And I know it's a lot to ask, but would it be possible for you to take me to my house in Chicago? I know it's a long drive, but we'll pay you for your time. My...my father is Senator Randall Ross."

She didn't want to play that card, but it was the only one she had left. And it was effective. The man's weather beaten face went slack and his mouth dropped open.

"Please, we've got to hurry!" she urged.

"Of course, I'm sorry. Of course I can help you. I'll get an ax and a crow-bar from the barn. My truck is over there." He motioned toward a large F-250 parked by the barn. "Get in and I'll be right there."

She and Danny ran to the truck and she wrenched open the door, giving him a boost so that he could get in. They waited impatiently until the farmer came back out carrying the tools. He also carried a long shotgun. Sydney's breath caught in her throat as he dropped everything into the bed of the truck and got in the driver's side door.

"Which way?"

Sydney pointed and he tore out of the driveway, dust from his driveway billowing out behind them.

"My name is Tom, by the way. Are you both okay, other than being scared?"

"We're fine now. I'm Sydney and this is Danny. He's my neighbor and he was just in the wrong place at the wrong time. He doesn't have anything to do with this mess. I need to get him safely back home."

She wrapped one arm around the slender little boy as she spoke.

"Don't worry about a thing, Sydney. I'll get you both safely back home."

Tom's confident tone made her believe him. Something about him reminded her of the old John Wayne movies that her dad liked to watch. She was still jittery, but sitting next to the old farmer was calming her nerves just a little bit at a time. He was big and strong and had a shotgun. She took a deep breath and tried to make her foot stop bouncing.

The truck roared down the deserted road and came upon the isolated little house in just a few minutes time. Sydney's heart started pounding again. The truck lurched to a stop amid clouds of dust and Sydney leaped out, with Tom and Danny close behind her.

As Sydney barged through the backdoor, she started calling Deidre's name. Deidre shouted back in relief as they led Tom to the door. The stench in the little house was so overpowering that it almost bowled them over. She briefly wondered why she didn't notice the smell the first night she was here, but put it out of her mind. She was probably in shock that night.

Tom knelt in front of the door and made quick work out of the padlock with his tools. Sydney decided wryly that having an ax made all the difference. She rubbed her raw feet as she watched him work. Within half a minute, the padlock and hinge dropped to the ground and the door swung open.

"Deidre?" Sydney called. "Come out. We're not going to hurt you. We've got to get out of here before he comes back."

Deidre didn't answer and she didn't come out and Sydney didn't have the patience to wait.

She crept into the doorway of the room and peered inside. Deidre was crouched in the back corner, eyeing the door cautiously, like a caged animal.

Sydney could tell that she was probably a pretty girl but her beauty was hidden behind quite a bit of grime and ugly harsh bruises. Her blondish-red hair was matted and tangled and she smelled horrible, like she had crawled straight out of the sewer.

Bright, suspicious green eyes peered out from under a layer of filth.

"Deidre?" Sydney said softly. "Come out. You're going to be safe now. But we have to leave here."

Deidre's face crumpled and she started sobbing. Sydney rushed into the room and put her arm around the distraught girl but the girl shirked away from her.

"Deidre, I know it is hard for you to believe right now, but I'm not going to hurt you. I promise. Now let's get you out of here before Harrison gets back."

The girl nodded and Sydney helped her hobble outside. It was clear to all of them that Deidre was in a bad way. She was very weak. Her clothes were ragged and her legs were covered in lash-like bruises.

Sydney winced as she saw the slashes on Deidre's back. It appeared as though she had been whipped. She swallowed hard as she tightened her grip on the injured girl. Tom and Danny led the way to the truck and they all piled inside.

Sydney turned to Tom.

"Thank you so much for helping us! Can you take us to my house, now? Please?"

She was hoping that Stephen would be at home. She desperately longed to hear his voice but she couldn't chance calling him. Harrison had probably tapped his phone.

"I know this is going to sound really stupid, but where are we?" She looked sheepish.

Tom didn't miss a beat, he just looked at her sympathetically.

"You're about ten miles east of Gary." That made sense. It had taken less than an hour to get from her house to the hide-away house the night she had been taken.

She settled back into the seat, leaning her head back and closing her eyes. She hadn't rested easily in a couple of weeks and the soft leather truck seat suddenly felt really good. Her eyes stung from lack of sleep. The hum of the road as they flew over it toward Chicago lulled her to sleep even in the midst of life-changing excitement. A body could only stay awake so long.

Awhile later, jolting bumps intruded into her peaceful sleep and she startled awake. She hadn't even been aware that she had fallen asleep. She jerked up in the seat to look out the window and was relieved to find that they were crossing the bridge on I94 into Chicago. She could see the Willis Tower rising out of the horizon which meant that she was almost home. Her close proximity to Stephen made her antsy all over again but she tried to ignore it. She couldn't make the truck go faster.

"I'm sorry I fell asleep," she apologized to Tom. I haven't slept much at all for weeks. I can't tell you how thankful I am that you helped us. I don't know what we would have done..."

He interrupted her. "Don't think a thing about it. I've never seen a sorrier looking pair than the two of you walking up my drive. I couldn't just go about my business, now could I?"

She smiled a jittery smile at him. She was on pins and needles. Would Stephen be home when they got there? What if he wasn't? What should they do? What should their next steps be? She took deep, calming breaths and focused on the road in front of them. It wouldn't do any good to fall apart now. Tom turned onto the Skyway and headed into town.

Fifteen minutes later, they pulled up in front of her house. Tom pulled the truck up behind Stephen's T-Bird before he turned to her.

"If you don't mind, I'll walk up with you to make sure that he's here." It was as if he had read her mind and discovered her secret fear…that Stephen wouldn't be home.

"Thanks, Tom."

She flashed a brief grin of relief at the kindly man before running up the sidewalk, her bloody feet barely touching the concrete. She didn't feel the pain, though. Or the exhaustion, fear and fatigue. All she knew was that she was just a scant twenty yards from the love of her life.

Before she even reached the door, it opened and Stephen filled the doorway, surprise and shock freezing him in place.

"Sydney?"

He opened his arms up just in time for her to leap into them, wrapping her legs around his waist. She buried her face into his neck and breathed him in. He smelled like soap and musk and Stephen. She was so relieved that she felt tears welling up in her eyes. After a minute, Stephen pulled his face back.

"Sydney, how are you here? Are you alright? What happened?"

He fired questions at her, one after the other, before she even had a chance to speak. And he didn't loosen his grip on her even a little bit. She smiled and pulled him close for just another second.

"Stephen, I love you so much. And I'll answer your questions, but not right now. There's no time. We've got to leave. We can't stay here. I'll explain in the car."

She unclasped her legs and dropped to the ground, wincing a little as pain shot from her feet up into her calves. She started to tug Stephen toward his car and then remembered Danny. He had trailed up the sidewalk behind her and was watching her now uncertainly.

She knew that his parents must be frantic with worry, but she was too afraid to turn him over to them right now... not with Harrison probably hot on their tail. All of a sudden, an idea occurred to her.

"This is going to sound crazy, but we need to get to my parents' house, I think. All of us."

Stephen did a double-take but she continued before he could interrupt.

"Danny, I know you miss your parents but you need to come with us for a little bit longer, okay? We can call your parents from a secure line."

The little boy nodded quickly, glancing wistfully at his house.

Tom stepped forward.

"Sydney, it isn't my place to say so, but won't the detective be looking for Stephen's car? Maybe I should just give you a ride on over to your parents' place. No one will be looking for Ol' Red."

He motioned to his big red truck as he spoke. "It might be safer and I'm happy to do it for you. It beats throwing hay bales around this afternoon." He grinned briefly before he started back toward his truck. "But you're right. We'd better move."

Luckily Stephen was dressed and he hesitated only long enough to lock the front door before he hurried behind them to the truck. They piled in and the heavy truck lurched forward toward Highland Park- a direction that Sydney hadn't thought she would travel toward for a very long time.

"Are you going to tell me what is going on now?" Stephen asked.

All the while, he had one arm around tightly around Sydney's shoulders, clutching him to her. Sydney never wanted him to let go of her again even if she did reek to high heaven.

"You're not going to believe it, but... here goes. Detective Daniels' had me kidnapped." She paused to let him absorb that information. His expression froze, along with the hand that had been lightly rubbing her back.

"Come again?" he asked politely, as though he hadn't heard her, but she knew that he had.

"Detective Daniels' is the one who took me. He's crazy. He just doesn't act like it."

"Oh my God," he muttered. "Sydney, he created a gag order forbidding anyone to tell the press that you had been taken. He said it was so they didn't accidentally alert your dad but really, it was to protect himself." He slapped a hand to his forehead. "How could I have been so stupid?"

"Stephen, seriously! No one in their right mind would have expected him to be the bad guy here. No one. This is not your fault. I certainly didn't see it coming."

"It's my fault that I didn't wake up when he took you." His voice was soft as he stared into her eyes.

She stared back incredulously.

"Stephen, I'm only going to tell you one more time because I mean it so completely. This is not your fault. None of it. The guy snatched me so fast that you couldn't have helped me even if you had heard. It wouldn't have been possible. But let me tell

you something else. It was you---
remembering *you* that gave me the strength
to kick down the door and escape."

"You kicked down a door?" The
incredulous look on his face made her smile.

"I know, hard to believe, right? It turns
out that I'm kind of self-sufficient."

She grinned good-naturedly, all the
while rubbing her dirty, bloody feet. She
wasn't sure that she would ever be able to
wear heels again, not that it mattered.

"Why, though? What did he want with
you?" Stephen stared at her, perplexed.

As Tom drove, she continued to tell
Stephen everything, including the part
where they had to return to the house to get
Deidre. By the time she had finished, she
was shaking-both from the memory and
from the feeling of immense relief that she
was safe.

"And I still don't know exactly how he
came up with using me to get to his step-
dad, but that's exactly what it is about," she
concluded. Stephen lifted her hand and
kissed it, then stared at it as it visibly shook.
He grasped it soothingly.

"Sydney, don't think about it anymore.
You're safe now. As far as I know, he hasn't
released that video to any news channel.

Yet. Maybe if we can get to your dad and explain everything… well, maybe he'll know what to do. But I just have to tell you — you are so brave that it blows my mind. I'm so proud of you!"

She leaned into the softness of his shirt and inhaled his clean scent. He wrapped his arms around her and she closed her eyes. She had been so afraid that she would never see him again. With his arms around her, she felt as though she was safe from the world. It was heaven.

She had barely closed her eyes before Stephen's voice penetrated her bubble of serenity.

"Sydney, what are we going to tell your parents?"

Her eyes snapped open. "The truth. My dad's got connections much higher than Detective Daniels does."

Tom smoothly pulled up to the gate of her parents' neighborhood and while the big red truck idled noisily, Sydney handed the guard on duty her identification. He examined it, handed it back and waved them through, although he did look at her curiously. She decided that she probably looked less than her best after not showering for two weeks.

She showed Tom where to turn and then nervously stared out the window as the luxurious homes passed her window. Each one of them was magnificent and a year ago, she wouldn't have thought twice about them. They were simply a part of her world. Now, as she passed them, she wondered fleetingly what kind of secrets the families inside of them were keeping. Because apparently, everyone had secrets. The world was not a simple place. There was no black and white, only varying shades of gray.

"Sydney…" Stephen's voice trailed off before he cleared his throat and tried again. "How do we know that we can trust your father?"

Tom pulled into her parents' cobblestone driveway at just that moment and Sydney stared up at the massive house looming in front of them.

"We don't."

CHAPTER TWELVE

The look on Jillian Ross' face was priceless when she answered the doorbell. She looked perfect, of course, in a pair of linen trousers and silk shell blouse. A multi-layered string of pearls adorned her neck and Sydney wondered for the hundredth time in her life if wearing pearls was a prerequisite for being a political wife. Her mother owned strings and strings of them.

"Well, look what the cat dragged in."

Jillian almost purred with bitter satisfaction as she stared at the bedraggled group in front of her. Her gaze flitted up and down the length of her daughter and the corner of her lip curled.

"Sydney, would it hurt you to shower? You might not live at home, but people still know who you are." She wrinkled her nose in disdain.

"Mom, can we come in? We have something extremely important to discuss with dad. It's absolutely critical."

Sydney hated pleading with her mother, but there was no way around it. Seeing the gloating expression on her mother's face was torturous.

"I told you that you would be back. But remember what I also told you. You aren't welcome here now. You made your bed. Now go lie in it."

Jillian started to close the door, but Stephen's hand flew out and firmly stopped it.

"Mrs. Ross, we really need to see your husband. I know that you are angry, but I also know that somewhere in your icy heart, you must love your daughter in your own way. This is a matter of life or death. Do you really want to risk your daughter's life? I'm not exaggerating in the slightest."

Jillian's mouth had formed a perfect O as Stephen spoke and as he finished, she snapped it closed.

"What do you mean life or death?" Stephen's dramatic statement had given her pause.

"I mean that we need to see Senator Ross. Right now."

Jillian silently gestured for them to come in and then led them through the house to the big mahogany doors of the senator's study. She knocked quickly before she entered. She didn't wait for him to answer.

"Rand, Sydney's here. With some...er, friends. They have something important to discuss with you, apparently."

She waved her thin hand toward them dismissively, her bored tone suggesting that she wasn't overly concerned or interested by their visit. Nonetheless, she remained to hear what they had to say.

Sydney pushed through the doors and stood in front of everyone else as her father rose from behind his desk and made his way across the room to them.

She had forgotten what a commanding person he was. A person could feel it, just standing near him. It emanated from him in an almost tangible way. Everything about him screamed *Powerful*.

Randall's face was instantly concerned as he took in the group in front of him, including his daughter's bedraggled state. Sydney knew that he was probably well aware that it took something earth shattering to get her back home. When he absorbed Deidre's bedraggled condition, the look on his face immediately changed to alarm as he turned to face his daughter.

"Sydney, what's wrong? What's going on here?"

At the concern in her father's voice, Sydney suddenly felt all of the emotions that she had been repressing over the last few weeks come rushing back to her at once. Her face crumpled and she began crying softly, her shoulders shaking.

Before Stephen could step forward to embrace her, her father had already moved. He pulled his daughter into his arms in the comforting way that only a father can. Sydney cried against his chest, soaking his Armani shirt as her father gently patted her back.

Stephen quickly explained the situation to her father. When he had finished, the look on Randall Ross' face was nothing short of murderous. He stepped away from Sydney and paced back toward his desk.

"That sick animal thought he could use you to get to me?" he thundered from across the room.

Sydney flinched. She had never seen her father lose his temper, not even once. He was usually too busy trying to pacify Jillian and being politically correct. But now his face was distorted in anger and a vein throbbed visibly at his temple.

"Not you so much, Daddy, as Paul Hayes." Sydney's voice seemed small in the cavernous room and she slipped right back into her familiar pattern of addressing her father as "daddy" without even realizing it.

"Apparently, Paul molested Harrison from the time he was small. I can tell you, Harrison is twisted now. He's crazy. And he's out to bring Paul down. You are just collateral damage to him because of your…involvement with Paul."

"My involvement with Paul?" Randall's face flickered with confusion before he was distracted by Danny.

"You haven't told me the significance of this boy, yet." He motioned to the boy, who was trying to hide behind Tom in the doorway.

"He was just in the wrong place at the wrong time. That's all. He tried to help me and now he's in danger, too. And maybe his parents are too. Maybe you should send someone to let them know the situation. And we definitely need to let them know that Danny's okay. I was afraid to do it while we were there because his parents don't realize that they can't trust Detective

Daniels. I didn't know how to convince them of that. His parents don't even know he's safe yet. And Deidre. Deidre needs help, dad. She doesn't know exactly how long Harrison kept her in that house, but he did horrible things to her. And she hasn't eaten in weeks."

As Sydney spoke, Deidre appeared to get even weaker, leaning into Stephen for support. Her dirty face was pale and she closed her eyes. Her knees shook and Randall's dark eyes scanned the girl's face before answering.

"Yes, I can see she needs help. I'm going to make some calls. Why don't you take little Danny upstairs so that you can get him cleaned up and maybe he would like a nap, as well. He looks dead on his feet." The senator smiled engagingly at the boy before returning his attention to Sydney.

"Stephen and Tom can stay down here with me and Deidre can go with your mother to the kitchen to get something to eat, before she cleans up. I think getting some nutrients in her is the most important thing. Also, I don't think it's a good idea for Tom to go back into that neighborhood just yet, do you?"

Tom broke in with his easy-going, country way.

"No, sir, I think you are probably right. I think I can rest here a spell while you folks figure things out." He grinned and squeezed Danny's shoulder. "Go on upstairs with Sydney, son. I think everything's going to be okay now."

Everyone began to file out of the study, but Randall grabbed Sydney's arm gently and pulled her back.

"Princess? I'm really sorry about…. well, everything. You're my only daughter and I haven't expressed it as much as I should have, but you are everything to me. I'm really glad that you came to me. And that you're safe. I feel horribly that I didn't even know you were in trouble. I'm sorry that I let you down. It won't happen again."

His face was sincere, his eyes misty. Sydney studied him for a moment before she leaned up and kissed him on the cheek.

"Thank you, daddy. I'm glad I'm here, too."

She turned and softly walked from the room, taking Danny's hand and leading him upstairs. His little gasps of shock as he absorbed his surroundings made her smile. It was odd, because now that she was back here after being at Stephen's, this grand house seemed much too excessive. It was large and perfect, like a museum. Much too perfect to actually live in.

She ran a bubble bath for Danny in a guest bathroom and left him to bathe while she went to soak in a hot bath of her own. Her bedroom was perfectly clean. Stella had picked up every article of clothing that Sydney had left strewn about when she had left in such a hurry. Everything was hanging neatly in the closet now. Sydney felt a twinge of guilt for being so spoiled back then. She had caused Stella quite a bit of unnecessary work.

She passed through her room and ran a bubble bath in the sunken marble tub. She quickly washed her hair under the faucet and then slathered conditioning balm on it, twisting it up on top of her head to keep it out of the water as she soaked. She lay back until she was chin deep in bubbles and closed her eyes. The feeling of washing away the grime of the past few weeks was heavenly.

After she had soaked for a good twenty minutes, she sat up again and scrubbed every inch of her body with a loofah. She felt the compulsive need to get rid of every trace of that little house. She rinsed her hair and then stepped out of the tub onto the thick bath mat. Her fingers looked like wrinkled prunes, but she didn't care. She was clean.

Her favorite skin care products were still lined up on the bathroom counter, so she liberally applied lotion to her arms and legs before she stepped into her closet to find something to wear. She opted for jeans and a simple t-shirt.

She only wanted to wear one piece of jewelry. A silver Tiffany bracelet that her father had given her once. The heart was engraved, "Princess." It was still in one of her massive jewelry boxes. She found it quickly and snapped it onto her wrist.

She used to think that her father didn't think the she was important enough to spend time with. But she had watched his face closely earlier. He was really upset by everything that had happened... and he did love her. Maybe it wasn't exactly the way she wanted it to be, but who really had exactly the relationship that they wanted with their parents?

A soft knock on her bedroom door interrupted her thoughts. Before she could get to the door to open it, her dad stuck his head in. She couldn't even remember the last time her father had come into her room, it had been so long.

"Sydney? Are you alright?" He asked in concern. "You've been up here a while."

"I'm fine. Now." She smiled warmly at him. "It feels so good to be clean and safe. Daddy, I really am sorry…. About everything. I've missed you."

As she spoke, she twisted her bracelet absently around her wrist.

"Sweetheart, I've missed you too."

Sydney's head snapped up in surprise. Her father had used an endearment. Had she completely misunderstood him all along?

He crossed her room and perched on the edge of her sofa, which made her smile. He looked completely out of place in her ultra-feminine room. Even though he was elegant for a man, his large frame looked a little like the Incredible Hulk sitting on her delicate couch.

"I've contacted the FBI. They're sending someone here and as soon as they arrive, we'll call for medical help for Deidre. We don't want to chance the ambulance calling in to the police until the FBI arrives. But Syd, while we wait, there's a couple of things I want to get off of my chest. Do you mind? It will only take a few minutes."

"Of course, Daddy."

Sydney situated herself so that she was squarely facing him, curiously waiting for him to continue speaking. Her leg bounced nervously. She hadn't been able to truly calm herself down yet. Her nerves didn't seem to realize that she was safe.

"I'm so sorry about not waiting to see you at the hospital. I let myself become influenced and went against my better judgment. But that is no excuse. I should have realized that even if you didn't think you wanted to see us, you still needed your parents during such a difficult time." He stared at her earnestly with genuine regret in his voice.

Sydney gaped at him.

"Why would you think that I didn't want to see you? I cried for months because I thought you didn't care. You never even contacted me to see where I was. For all you knew, I was in a homeless shelter. And if it weren't for Stephen, I would have been. When I left, mom closed my bank accounts. I had no money. You wouldn't even have known if I had starved to death!"

Randall stared at her in shock.

"Sydney, what are you talking about? Your mom didn't close your bank accounts. And you spoke with your mother several times. We knew where you were. You told your mother that you hated us and didn't want to see us."

Even though he stated it as a fact, his voice was suddenly unsure.

"Didn't you?"

"Um, no. And yes, mom most certainly did close my bank accounts. I left with $85 dollars in my pocket and that was all I had. She told me that if I took my car with me, she would report it as stolen. And I didn't hear a word from either one of you until mom came to see me at the cafe and told me to come home. You know… after the text incident."

Sydney realized that her voice had gradually crept up a couple of octaves and made a conscious effort to calm down.

"What text incident?" Randall's brow was wrinkled and he seemed as confused as Sydney felt.

"The text that you accidentally sent to me instead of to Paul Hayes. Surely you remember."

"Sydney, I have no idea what you are talking about." Her father's voice was firm.

"I haven't texted you in months. Accidentally or otherwise. Your mother felt that we should respect your wishes and not contact you until you had gotten all of your resentment out of your system. She thought that would be for the best."

"My mother. Okay, things aren't making sense here."

The wheels were spinning in Sydney's head and she couldn't quite put the puzzle pieces together.

"It seems to me that mom has been lying to you. Nothing she told you was true."

"It appears that you are right, but to what end? Why would she want to drive a wedge between us?" Her father was genuinely puzzled, that much was apparent.

"Daddy, this is really embarrassing and I don't want to ask... but..are you gay?"

Sydney forced the uncomfortable words out, trying not to blush. It didn't work. Her cheeks were flaming.

Randall Ross went completely still, his face impassive as he stared at the floor in front of him. After a minute, he asked stiffly, "Why would you ask that?"

"That was the text. It was a text that appeared to be from you to Paul Hayes, only you sent it to me instead. If you didn't send it, someone with access to your Blackberry must have. That leaves your assistant or... mom. But why would she do that?" Sydney was beyond confused.

"No, I'm not gay."

Her dad squared his shoulders and looked her in the eye.

"This is not a conversation that I ever thought I would have with you. But it appears to be necessary now."

He took a deep breath and started talking, gazing into space as if he was seeing his memories unfold in front of him. He twisted his thick gold wedding band absently all the while.

"Another Senator came onto me, a very good friend... months and months ago. We had spent a lot of time together trying to draft up a bill that we both felt strongly about.

"One night, after we had worked too late into the night and had one too many drinks, he tried to kiss me after we walked out of a restaurant. I rebuffed him, of course, but a picture was taken. The photographer has been blackmailing me ever since. I wasn't a willing participant in that... embrace, but the picture sure makes it look like I was."

"Was the senator Paul Hayes?" Sydney asked softly.

"Yes, it was Paul. And even though I've been very angry with him for crossing the line and wreaking so much havoc on me with the blackmailing photographer, the Paul that I know would never victimize a child in the way that you described. I just can't bring myself to believe it. It doesn't make any sense."

The utter look of bewilderment and betrayal on her father's face broke Sydney's heart. So she changed the subject.

"How does mom fit into all of this? Why has she lied about me? Why do you think she let me think that you were gay?"

"I don't know," Randall admitted, his eyes stark. "Your mother and I haven't been very happy together for a long time, as you probably know. Even though parents try to hide things from their children, children are usually smart enough to see through it. Your mother and I have grown apart. Although, she stood with me on paying the photographer who was blackmailing me. It would have ruined my career."

"And it still will."

Jillian's ice-cold voice came from the doorway. "Well, that and the minor fact that you are going to murder your own daughter today."

Both Randall and Sydney whipped around to stare at her. Jillian stood with one hand on her hip and the other holding a gleaming black handgun. Sydney gasped as her mother's stormy blue eyes rained hatred at both of them. Sydney instinctively recoiled from it.

"Murder my own daughter? What the hell are you talking about, Jillian?"

Randall lurched to his feet and challenged his wife without fear, regardless of the gun in her hand. But Jillian ignored his question.

"How does it feel, Rand?" Jillian almost sang as she sauntered gracefully forward. Sydney couldn't stop staring as her mother drew to a stop in front of Randall. She suddenly found it very difficult to breathe.

Randall glared at Jillian. "How does what feel?"

"How does it feel to have everything crash down around you?" Jillian smiled a sadistic smile, giving Sydney goose bumps. She had always known that her mother was unfeeling, even cold. But Sydney had not ever been aware that her mother was such an evil, calculating bitch.

"What is your plan, Jillian?" Randall's voice was just as cold as his wife's. "You know that if anything happens to me, life as you know it is over. Is that really what you want?"

"Oh, Randall. Don't worry about little ol' me. I'll land on my feet. I've been investing money of my own for a long time and so I'm quite wealthy now, if I do say so myself. Even without your money."

"Then you also know that when we divorce, I'll get half of your investments." Randall smiled a tired smile. "Maybe you're not as smart as you think you are."

"That would only be true if you were alive to divorce me. But unfortunately, Randall, that won't be the case. Didn't you notice my little friend here?"

She made a circle in the air with her gun.

"I'll be collecting your life insurance instead. Much more lucrative. Of course, that will only be after you kill Sydney. I'm a greedy bitch, I admit it."

Randall's face went slack as he realized what she was saying.

"This is about money? Jillian, think about this. There is no way that you will get away with anything. I've already called the FBI. They're on the way."

She laughed a casual, tinkling laugh.

"Oh, sweet, naïve Randall. Don't worry. We have a plan. Well, I guess I should say we have a *new* plan. When Sydney arrived here today with her little entourage, it threw a wrench in our original plan. But we think our new one will turn out nicely. You and Paul are going to turn on us all and we're going to have to defend ourselves."

"*We* have a plan? Who is *we*, mother?"

Sydney tried to keep her voice from shaking, but the shock of everything was bearing down on her quickly.

"Now, Sydney, I thought you were smarter than that—that you had it all figured out. You were smart enough to escape Harrison, weren't you? Come on-put the pieces together. I want to watch your face when you figure it out."

Jillian's taunting voice didn't hold even a shred of maternal love for her daughter. It turned Sydney's stomach. Realization dumped on her like cold water and she sucked her breath in.

"You're with Harrison. You've been in on it from the beginning. You wanted me dead. Why?"

"Well, Sydney. That whole kidnapping thing was your own fault. If you had only decided to release a video to the press as Harrison had suggested, then I wouldn't have had to draw you into this. But once we had to kidnap you to get it, you sealed your own fate. It's a good thing I doubled your life insurance when I doubled your father's years ago."

She glanced sideways at Sydney.

"That was good foresight, I will admit." Her crimson tipped talon-like fingers gripped her gun tighter as she faced them.

"Mom," Sydney interrupted frantically. "You really intend to kill your own family?"

"I've never been much of a mother, have I, Sydney? This shouldn't surprise you too much. My marriage was a lie from the very beginning. Your father only wanted me as a decoration for his arm. And then to find out that he has been gay this entire time? That was a slap in the face that was just too much for me to bear. But lucky for me, as far as anyone else knows, we're still a perfect, All-American family. Watch this!"

She quickly contorted her face into sobbing, as real tears streamed down her face.

"Oh my God...What will I do now? My family was my life. I wish it had been me instead! If only I had known that Randall was involved with such a monster... Maybe I could have helped. But now... it's too late. They're gone...my precious baby Sydney..."

Her voice trailed off as she began wailing heaving sobs. Then she abruptly stopped and grinned at her daughter and husband with wet lashes and a devious smile.

"Convincing, right?"

Sydney stared at her mother in disbelief. She was just as crazy as Harrison.

"Our marriage wasn't a lie, Jillian. You know that I'm not gay. I'm sorry that you didn't feel appreciated in our marriage, but that is no reason to call it a lie. You and I were in love once."

Randall kept his voice calm as he tried to reason with his wife. Sydney didn't miss the fact that he had subtly moved in front of her as if shielding her from Jillian. She appreciated the gesture, but didn't figure that it made much difference at this point.

"Yes, once. We were in love and everything was perfect. But then you started dilly-dallying with your assistants and you never made time for me and I finally realized that you never really loved me at all."

Jillian sounded tortured for a brief moment before she steeled her tone again. Randall sighed, as if they'd had this same conversation a hundred times before.

"I did love you, Jillian. I wouldn't have married you if I didn't. We simply grew apart, and that happens sometimes. You didn't want to put the work in to get our relationship back—you just wanted to order me to love you again. And that doesn't work."

"Save it Randall. Just save it. You know that we couldn't have gone to counseling because that would have leaked to the press. I've wasted more tears on you than I should have. And trust me, I haven't cried over you in a long, long time."

"Okay, Jillian. I hear you. You're upset with me- you hate me. That's fine. Maybe I deserve that. But our daughter... Jillian, she didn't ask for any of this. You should let her go. Right now."

"I can't, Randall. How in the world would I go about that? It's too late. She shouldn't have gotten pregnant and caused me a headache. If you think about it, she really brought all of this on herself. And so did you, Rand. If you had only loved me like you should have, I wouldn't have been forced to turn to *him*."

Jillian's voice turned to a whimper and Sydney's heart felt as though it had stopped beating as she realized the extent of her mother's delusion.

Her mother's glittering blue eyes had lost any semblance of logic or reason. Instead, they had the glazed-over gleam of a psychopath. Panic overwhelmed her as she glanced at the door. She kept expecting help to arrive at any minute, but so far the door frame had remained empty.

"Are you expecting someone, Syd?" Her mother's smile was malicious. "I wouldn't. While you were taking your leisurely soak, I put a sedative in everyone's tea. They're peacefully sleeping while we wait for Harrison to arrive with Paul. Don't worry, no one will feel a thing. They won't even wake for their last breaths."

Jillian laughed a maniacal laugh as Sydney's heart started furiously skipping beats.

"Not Stephen. Right, mother? You haven't hurt Stephen?"

Jillian only laughed and Sydney's shoulders slumped as all hope abandoned her. The love of her life was dead or very close to it. She had lived through a kidnapping only to be murdered by her own mother for which her father was going to be framed shortly before being murdered himself.

This couldn't be happening. But it was.

CHAPTER THIRTEEN

"Drink it." Jillian thrust a heavy glass at Sydney.

They were standing in the cheerful, sunny kitchen, after Jillian had forced Sydney and her father downstairs at gunpoint. The atmosphere was anything but cheerful, however.

Jillian's expression was murderous and Sydney's stomach was quivering now to the point that she thought she was going to vomit. Randall seemed as though he was on the verge of strangling his wife regardless of the gun in her hand. He wasn't accustomed to being rendered powerless.

"No." Sydney shook her head.

"Drink it." Jillian repeated through gritted teeth. "You won't like the consequences if you don't."

"Or what, mother? Will you kidnap me? Too late. You've already done that. Will you kill me? Oh, wait- you're going to do that anyway. You just want to do it when I can't look you in the eyes. If you want to kill me, do it now. I want to be awake for my last breath."

Sydney couldn't keep the sarcasm and bitterness out of her voice as she stared her mother right in the eyes. She was exhausted, her mother was going to kill her and she was terrified that Jillian had already killed Stephen. This was the mother of all bad days.

"Jillian," Randall began. "You don't have to do this. You really don't. So much has gone unsaid over the years that I think that it's just gotten out of hand. How about... you and I go somewhere alone and discuss this?"

Jillian looked at him as though he had lost his mind. Sydney had to wonder herself what in the world her dad had hoped to accomplish. Obviously, Jillian had come too far now. There was no way she could let either of them live. And she was beyond reasoning with. That much was clear.

Before anyone could say another word, voices approached the kitchen and Sydney tensed in anticipation. Maybe Stephen was alright after all. Was he hunting for her?

Her eyes were frozen on the doorway as her breath caught in her throat. But her hope died yet again as Harrison's lean body entered the room, shoving a very frightened looking and rumpled Senator Paul Hayes in front of him. The senator had a large bruise forming on his left cheek and there was dried blood on the corner of his swollen lip as he nervously looked around the room.

"Get over there, *dad*," Harrison sneered as he shoved his step-father toward Randall and Sydney. Paul stumbled over his own shoe and Randall reached out to steady his elbow.

"Paul, are you alright? They're saying horrible things about you. That you did unspeakable things."

The uncertainty was obvious on Randall's handsome face as he pulled his hand away from Paul's arm and watched him for a response.

"Randall, you have to believe me. These two are sick! I didn't touch him. I'm not a pervert. I would never touch a child- it's ludicrous. You know me, I wouldn't. But they're behind that picture... the one that you were so angry with me about? Harrison hired that photographer. And that's my fault because I crossed the line that night. I'm sorry, Randall."

The anguished look on Paul's battered face was so sincere, that Sydney believed him in an instant. His eyes were kind and tortured as he gazed at Randall. Sydney could tell that her father believed him, as well. The relief on his face was visible to anyone.

"It doesn't matter now, does it, lovebirds?" Harrison growled. "The truth, that is. The only thing that matters now is the truth that the public hears. *My* truth. And that truth is that you were having an illicit affair. We have pictures to prove it. My old man molested me for years and was quite sick. He even had a secret house on the edge of Gary to hold victims in. Such as the poor girl, Deidre."

"Yes, poor Deidre," Jillian purred. "You're a sick, sick man, Paul."

She stood on the edge of the group, her gun held loosely in her hand as she observed the scene in front of her. She almost seemed amused.

"You make quite a team," Randall stated, as though he were bestowing a compliment. "You know, it is clear to me why my wife would be involved in this. But why you, Harrison? What have we done to *you* to deserve any of this?"

"Why do you feel as though you deserve an explanation?" Harrison asked, as he leaned casually against the marble counter. "Although it should be obvious. Last year, when my dear step-father found out that he has cancer, he changed his will. And I'm not in it."

"You have cancer?" Randall turned to Paul in astonishment, who appeared resigned as he nodded tiredly.

"I didn't want to upset anyone yet. There was no sense in it, since there isn't anything that anyone can do. It's untreatable. The doctor gave me a year at the most."

"Yes, a year. And a year isn't very long to stage this whole thing. But we managed to pull it off, didn't we, Jillian?"

She nodded at Harrison in satisfaction, not taking her gun off of the group as she beamed at her accomplice.

"But I still don't understand why." Randall persisted. "Why did you want to stage all of this? He already took you out of the will. What will you accomplish by killing him? Revenge?"

"How can a US senator be so stupid? I'm embarrassed by our elected officials, truly." Harrison shook his head.

"I needed to stage this in order to make my mother feel sorry for me—that her poor son was so traumatized by having his dear step-father molest him for years and then turn on him that she will leave everything to me with a little bit of gentle persuasion. It won't take much. She'll be overcome with guilt for allowing such abuse to happen under her nose. And then, of course, I'll kill her, as well."

"I can't believe that any one person can possibly be so heinous." Randall glared at him.

"You don't know the half of it, daddy." Sydney interjected. "He's an evil person. He kept Deidre locked up for God knows how long, raping her every day, not feeding her. Mother, you really know how to pick them. How did you two find each other, anyway?"

For some strange reason, she felt a sense of calm as she faced her mother. It wasn't like they could do much more to her. Her death warrant was already signed.

Sydney was surprised to see that for the first time, Jillian looked slightly unsure of herself. She ignored Sydney's question and glanced at Harrison.

"Is that true? Did you really have sex with that girl? You didn't mention that."

"*That's* the part that bothers you, mother? That he *raped* her while he held her against her will, beat her and starved her? You don't care that he is plotting to murder your family and then his own mother? All you care about is that he had sex with someone other than you?"

Sydney didn't know if she could feel any more astounded than she already did. Her mother truly was a monster. Harrison interrupted them in annoyance.

"Does it really matter, Jillian? Fate threw us together and we spit in its face by creating our own destiny out of the shit that we were dealt. Everything is going off without a hitch. And in a couple of weeks, we'll leave here together, and never look back."

Harrison's cobalt eyes glittered coldly as he spoke, as he turned to face his accomplice. He reached out to grasp her arm, but she jerked away and took a step back.

"But you didn't tell me. About the girl. That matters to me." Jillian stared at him.

"For God's sake, Jillian. I can't see why that would matter. She was just a whore that I dated a few times."

"Yes, a whore that you apparently couldn't live without. You kept her under lock and key for God only knows how long. Maybe you knew that if you didn't lock her up, eventually she would leave you when she figured out that you're a *monster*." Sydney couldn't help but to interrupt again, but Jillian wasn't paying attention.

"It matters because I can't trust you." Her voice hardened.

Before anyone could react, Jillian aimed her gun squarely at his chest and pulled the trigger at point-blank range without hesitation.

Harrison's expression was astounded as he staggered backward against the granite counter. "You bitch!"

He pressed his hands to his chest as if to compress the bleeding, but it couldn't possibly help. The blood spurted over and around his hands like a fountain, quickly soaking through his pale gray shirt.

He started to say something else, but blood gurgled from his mouth before he could form the words. He crumpled to the floor into a crimson pool, which quickly saturated the rest of his expensive clothing.

Sydney couldn't breathe as she stared at the bloody body in front of her. Harrison's eyes stared lifelessly straight ahead, seemingly right at her, so she closed her own to shut the image out.

"That fool. As if I could have let him live anyway." Jillian actually smiled as she stared at Harrison's twitching body. "Can't you just see the headlines now? 'Senator's wife is the sole survivor in a twisted love triangle gone bad. Heroic detective dies in an effort to save her.'"

Chapter
Fourteen

Stephen's hand twitched, then twitched again. He was slowly waking up, which he found curious because he hadn't realized that he had gone to sleep.

He was lying flat on his back on the floor, which was also strange because he had no idea how he got there. The thick carpet against his back wasn't unpleasant however, so he remained still for a moment, trying to grasp what had happened. His memory was blank.

His eyelids were heavy and when he finally managed to get them open, the room surrounding him was blurry. He squeezed his eyes shut and re-opened them with only slightly better results. There seemed to be two of everything. The deep yellow color on the walls seemed to create a golden haze around him as everything blurred together.

He had been drugged. That much was obvious. A memory came rushing back to him.

A fancy china teacup.

He thought harder, focusing on that teacup. Jillian had brought both he and Tom hot tea earlier. He didn't remember anything after that. So, it was the tea. Thankfully, he had only taken a few sips of it. Judging by how woozy he felt right now, whatever was in it had been very strong. If he had finished the cup, it might have killed him.

Across the room, in a plush wing-backed chair next to the fireplace, Tom sat with his head tilted straight back and his mouth hanging open. He was snoring loudly with a tea cup spilled in his lap. His wrinkled, calloused hand had dropped to the floor.

Stephen scanned the room with blurry vision. He and Tom were the only two people in the room. He heaved his body up into a crouched position, holding his head in his hands for a scant minute while he regained his balance.

He sat still, listening for noises coming from the rest of the house. There was nothing. He had no idea how long he had been out, but sunshine poured in through the windows so it was still afternoon. He didn't allow himself to be comforted by that. Quite a lot could have happened in an hour or even a few minutes. The quiet surrounding him was eerie and it completely unnerved him. It made the large house seem like a mausoleum.

As quickly as he could, he pushed himself off of the floor into a standing position, leaning heavily onto the senator's massive desk for balance.

His eyes focused in on the senator's desk phone. He picked it up. Thankfully, there was a dial tone. He realized that he hadn't been expecting one. He pushed the redial button with a shaking finger. The effects of the drug were wreaking havoc on him. He could barely even think straight.

"This is Briggs," a male voice answered.

"Is this the FBI?" Stephen whispered as softly as he could while still being audible.

"Yes. This is Agent Briggs. Who is this?"

"This is Stephen James. I'm calling from Senator Randall Ross' desk phone. He said that he called you earlier?"

"Yes, he did. We're en route to his property. We should arrive within fifteen minutes."

"That might be too late. I don't know what is going on, but Jillian Ross drugged me and it looks like everyone else, too. I don't know the whereabouts of the senator, his wife or his daughter. But I do know that everyone here is in danger. It looks like Mrs. Ross is involved in whatever is going on. Just hurry."

Without waiting for a response, Stephen replaced the receiver into the cradle of the phone. His only purpose was to make the FBI was aware of the situation. Now that they were, he could focus on the most important thing.

Finding Sydney.

He crept as silently as he could across the room, checking Tom's pulse. It was steady and strong. He shook the older man gently in an effort to wake him, but Tom wouldn't rouse. Stephen gave up and continued on to the doorway. He glanced down the long hallway, but saw nothing unusual. Until he stepped out and almost tripped on Deidre. She was lying directly parallel with the wall right outside of the office doorway.

Kneeling beside her, he rolled her over. But even before he could check for a pulse, he knew that she was dead. Her skin was still warm, but her green eyes were unfocused and fixated lifelessly on the wall. He drew in a ragged breath before tucking her hair behind her ear and closing her eyes softly. There were no marks or blood visible on her, so he had to assume that her degenerated system had absorbed all of the drug that Jillian had fed her and it had killed her.

As he stared at her battered face, a wave of compassion flooded through him at the end that this poor girl had met. She had fought for God only knows how long as Harrison's captive, enduring emotional and physical abuse, only to be killed by drinking a cup of tea.

Adrenaline and fury began pumping through him and he lunged to his feet, charging down the stairway. His vision was still fuzzy but he disregarded it. He'd have to make it work- he was intent on finding Sydney before Deidre's fate became hers as well.

He turned left at the end of the hall and cautiously opened the first door that he came to. And the question of the whereabouts of the Ross' staff was answered. The bodies of Stella and Ben were draped over the edge of a bathtub.

Blood ran down Stella's arm, forming a pool on the floor by the marble tub. His heart accelerated into a sprint. The body count was up to three. Apparently, Jillian was planning on leaving no witnesses.

He tried to plot a course of action in his head, but the drug in his system was making his thought process sluggish. It was frustratingly hard to think and he shook his head to clear it.

As he concentrated, he suddenly remembered seeing a shot gun in the bed of Tom's truck. Since he was only steps from the front door, he quietly slipped outdoors and made his way to the truck, trying to keep out of sight of any of the house windows. He had no way of knowing who might be watching.

Rounding the bed of the truck, he spotted a battered old shotgun with relief. He lifted it out, flipped it open and found that it was loaded.

Unfortunately, Tom hadn't brought any replacement ammunition. Stephen would have to make do with two rounds, which was better than nothing. He grasped the cool metal tightly as he climbed the stone stairs of the front porch. It didn't even occur to him to run and save himself. His only thought was of finding Sydney.

As he stepped quietly into the foyer, he caught the faint sound of voices coming from the back end of the house. He silently cursed the fact that he had never been in the house before. He was completely unfamiliar with it. Lifting the gun up onto his shoulder, he crept slowly into the direction of the muffled voices, his nerves standing up on end. He would just have to follow the noise.

As he continued stealthily through the library, the voices got infinitely sharper and more defined. Jillian's hateful voice drifted through the room to him.

"Honestly, Sydney. You act as though you've never seen a dead person before! Well, I guess you hadn't, but you can cross that off your bucket-list now. You're welcome."

Jillian laughed bitterly and Stephen felt relief flood through him in warm waves. Sydney was alive. That was all that mattered.

He crossed the remainder of the large room in four strides and chanced a glance into the kitchen. He found Jillian with her back facing him standing over the bloody, inert body of Harrison Daniels. He wasn't sorry to see Harrison in the position that he was in, but his comfort was short-lived. Jillian was armed.

His gaze flew to Sydney's face. She was slumped into her father's side, as pale as he had ever seen her. But she was alive. He couldn't see any visible injuries, making him want to sing and shout, but his relief died quickly.

"Okay. Who wants to go next?"

Jillian swung the gleaming black gun around, pointing it at each of them in turn. Sydney, Randall and Paul stared at her motionlessly, each face expressionless.

The kitchen lights reflected off of a slight sheen of perspiration glazing Senator Hayes' forehead, which was the only give-away of his distress. By all other appearances, they were utterly calm. No one in the group noticed Stephen's head poking into the doorway. He felt his heart pound as he tried to decide what to do.

He had two rounds of ammunition and Jillian was only one person. But she was standing directly in front of the group. The spray from the shot gun could hit any of them.

"Oh, come on. I've had my practice round out of the way. It'll be quick, I promise." Jillian laughed again as she grabbed Sydney by the hair.

"Why don't you go, *princess?* Ladies first. And after you're gone, dear daddy won't have anything to live for anyway."

"You're a sick bitch, you know that?" Paul muttered.

"Oh, I'm the sick one? You're the one who had an affair with a married man! For *years.* All while living a lie to the public...you had a perfect wife, perfect kids, perfect family. Perfect *lies.* Oh and let's not forget, *you're* the one who molested poor Harrison his whole life."

"Those are lies and you know it!" Paul protested, his hands clenched into tight fists at his sides.

"Yes," Jillian answered smoothly, "I do know. But the rest of America won't."

She paused to grin at him like a sick Cheshire cat.

"The best lies are those that are combined with truths. It makes them much more believable. Isn't it crazy that your *lies* about your sexuality are going to make it seem plausible that you're a monster? Because once the public learns that you tried to hide who you are, they'll believe that anything is possible. Because you lied about everything else."

She cackled crazily as she stared at Paul's appalled face.

"Ignore her." Randall instructed him calmly. "She's beyond reason now."

Randall focused on Jillian. "Jillian, at least let me hug Sydney one more time. Will you do that? It's not too much to ask. "

As he spoke, he leveled his gaze at Stephen and Stephen realized that the senator was entirely aware of his presence. His breathing quickened as he watched carefully for Randall's next move.

"Oh, whatever. You're a sentimental fool."

Jillian shoved Sydney hard into Randall. He caught her easily and hugged her close, keeping his eyes on his wife.

"Get behind me," he whispered.

"What?" Sydney pulled away from him in surprise, but he grabbed her and thrust her behind him before she had time to react. He guarded her with his body as he addressed his wife again.

"You're the fool. And you're going to have to shoot me first, Jillian. It won't look like I shot my own daughter, I can guarantee you that." His expression was grim as he continued to shield his daughter.

"Stop, Randall. I *will* shoot you. I don't want to do it this way, but I will." Jillian's voice was venomous and didn't falter. The gun she aimed at him did not shake in the slightest.

"Well, darling, what way do you plan on doing it? Did you plan on kneeling next to me and whispering endearments? I think not." Randall almost sounded as though he was taunting her. Jillian narrowed her eyes.

"Hmm. You know, if you're going to make things difficult..."

Jillian's voice trailed off as she changed the aim of her gun. She swung it around until it was pointed at Paul Hayes' heart.

"We'll just do it this way."

Paul only had time to gasp before Jillian calmly squeezed the trigger and he staggered backward, crashing through a window. Randall's shout split the air. Time seemed to stand still as they all watched Senator's Hayes' body roll to a stop on the ground outside and remain unmoving.

"He's dead because of you," Jillian hissed.

"No!"

Randall broke the silence and lunged forward like a cannon, grabbing Jillian and spinning her around. She struggled against him, but he moved with the strength of a raging bull and he was much larger than she was. With one hand, he forced Jillian's gun straight up in the air. With the other, he held her slim body tightly to his chest.

"Now!" he yelled to Stephen. "Do it now!" He glanced at Sydney. "Syd, get back!"

Jillian screeched wildly, flailing like a maniac. In the midst of the struggle, her gun went off, shooting a hole in the ceiling. Randall grasped her hand tighter, squeezing until her knuckles turned white. Sydney looked in relief at Stephen before she moved away from her parents.

Stephen didn't waste another second. He stepped into the doorway, took quick aim and shot Jillian squarely in the chest. The impact sent both she and Randall flying backward into the breakfast bar, sending the bar stools flying into every direction.

Sydney screamed as blood splattered onto her. She wasn't sure whose blood it was because the entire kitchen seemed to be a scene from a bloody nightmare. Her feet slipped and slid in the pooled blood on the floor and she tripped and fell backward. Everything was happening in slow motion.

Her mother hit the ground and flopped over face down. She lay still as her blonde hair quickly became saturated with her own blood as it pooled around her. Her gun rested limply in her motionless hand.

Randall lay beside her, his breathing hard and labored, but his eyes open. Sydney rushed to his side, pausing only to kick her mother's gun across the kitchen floor. She tried not to notice that her father's hand was covered in blood as she grasped it tightly to her chest. She swallowed hard and focused on her dad's face.

"Daddy, please. Don't die. please," she pleaded as Randall closed his eyes.

"I'm trying not to, princess," he whispered, but he didn't re-open his eyes. She gripped his hand even tighter.

He struggled to speak. "Is Paul…"

Sydney swallowed hard and glanced at Paul. He was laying completely still outside of the window. The shattered window was spattered with blood and she didn't see Paul's chest moving. She didn't think he was breathing.

"I don't know, daddy. I can't tell," she murmured.

Even she could detect the doubt in her voice, however. Randall nodded almost imperceptibly. Sydney felt Stephen's presence directly behind her before she felt him lightly grasp her shoulder.

Glancing up at him, she asked hurriedly, "Stephen, can you call an ambulance, please?"

She let go of her father's hand only to use her own to try and staunch the bleeding from the wound in her father's shoulder. She gasped as she saw how much blood pumped out around her hand. He was losing far too much blood.

"Daddy, you're going to be fine," she insisted. She wasn't sure if she was assuring herself or Randall. She began praying so quickly that it sounded like a mantra.

"Please, God. Please, please, God." She couldn't even manage to finish the prayer. She knew that God would know what she was praying for. And she just kept repeating it. "Please, God. Please, please..."

She could hear Stephen speaking on the kitchen phone, rushing his words as he requested an ambulance. At the exact same time, she heard loud footsteps charging through the house and men yelling "FBI!"

She didn't feel any relief, however, because she could feel her father's life slipping from him and his body starting to shake.

"Please, daddy. Don't die..."

Chapter Fifteen

The fact that she should be devastated didn't escape her. Her mother was lying in a pool of blood in front of her, but somehow Sydney couldn't bring herself to react. She knew that it would hit her later. All of the pain from her mother's betrayal and hatred would sink in when this was all over, but for now, she only felt numb.

She stood silently in the corner of the kitchen with Stephen's arm wrapped around her shoulder, watching the paramedics work on her father. He was on a gurney now, strapped to an oxygen mask and an IV bag. The paramedics were working so fast that their hands seemed to be a blur. He was still alive, though, and that was the important thing.

Paul Hayes was not. Neither were Ben Keyes, Stella Wilkinson, Harrison Daniels, Deidre Wilcox or Jillian Ross. Six lives had been taken in one afternoon. It seemed like she should feel differently now that the balance of life had shifted so much directly in front of her. But she still only felt the strange numbness consuming her. It all felt almost surreal.

She sank to the floor and Stephen sat next to her. Someone brought her a blanket and she didn't bother telling them that she wasn't cold. She was shaking from the shock. Stephen wrapped it around her shoulders anyway and held her hand.

"Sydney, I'm so sorry. This shouldn't have happened. Tell me what to do and I'll do it."

His voice was pained and it caught in his throat. She turned her watery hazel eyes to stare at him, blankly at first and then with compassion.

"Stephen, none of this is your fault. I'm alive because of you. My dad is alive because of you. Thank you. You saved me. Again." She leaned into his shoulder, resting her head against him. "I love you."

"I love you, too," he murmured back, rubbing her shoulders lightly. She closed her eyes, enjoying the comfort that she found in his touch. His were hands that would never hurt her.

"Sydney?" They both looked up in surprise at the tiny voice.

"Danny! Where have you been?"

With everything that had happened, Sydney had completely forgotten about the little boy. She hadn't seen him since she left him in the bath tub. It seemed like ages ago now.

Danny was incredibly pale as he stood silently in the doorway, taking in the bloody scene in front of him. It took a moment before Sydney realized that blood was running down his arm and dripping onto the floor in droplets. She jumped up and rushed to him, pulling him down onto her lap on the floor so that she could examine him.

"Danny, what happened?"

"I don't know. I was upstairs, resting after your mom gave me a snack and tea. And then a little bit ago, a bug bit me. And I started bleeding."

A bug bite? Stephen and Sydney's eyes met over the little boy's head, and in unison, they looked at the hole in the ceiling.

Jillian's errant bullet. The guest bedroom that Danny had been in was directly over the kitchen. Sydney quickly pushed Danny's sleeve up to his shoulder to find an inch-long cut on his bicep. The bullet had only grazed him although it might be deep enough to require stitches. All of the breath in her lungs exhaled in a whoosh of relief.

She hugged him tightly to her.

"Danny, I'm so sorry that you got mixed up in all of this. So, so sorry. If you go with Stephen, he can take you to call your parents, okay? And then a paramedic will have to look at your arm."

She hugged him again and then handed him off to Stephen. "I've got to check on my dad."

She stepped carefully through the mess in the kitchen. It was like a warzone. Jillian and Harrison's bodies were outlined by tape and tiny flags. FBI agents were busily taking samples and photographing the scene. Shattered glass and pools of blood seemed to be everywhere, so Sydney carefully watched where she stepped, although she tried to avoid looking at her mother's body.

The paramedics finally seemed to have her father ready to transport to the hospital, so Sydney stepped up to his side. His olive complexion was drained of color and his eyes were closed. She grabbed his hand.

"Daddy?"

Randall Ross opened his eyes and looked at his daughter. She felt the weakness in his grasp as he squeezed her hand. Anxiety creased her brow as she stared down at him.

"Sydney, I'm going to be fine. It's a shoulder wound. They've stopped the bleeding and everything is going to be okay. I love you."

A lump formed in her throat that she found extremely difficult to swallow.

"I love you, too, Daddy. We'll see you at the hospital."

Two paramedics began pushing him rapidly toward the door, so Sydney took a step back to allow them to pass. She was still standing in the same spot a few minutes later, lost in her thoughts, when FBI Agent Briggs approached her.

Short and middle-aged, Briggs was nondescript in appearance. Without his blue jacket with the yellow "FBI" letters, she would never have guessed who he was. But his eyes were kind.

"Miss Ross?" He seemed hesitant to interrupt her reverie. She offered him a small smile and extended her hand with all of the grace of Jackie O.

"Agent. Thank you for coming here to help."

He reached out and shook her hand.

"I'm sorry that we couldn't get here sooner. The courage that you've shown is admirable, young lady."

"Thank you," she murmured softly, still looking absently around the room. "There are so many things about today that I'm never going to understand."

"I can imagine." Agent Briggs solemnly evaluated her bloodied face, not a drop of which was her own. "Well, actually, maybe I can't. You've gone through hell. Anyone who thinks that money can buy happiness should come and talk to you."

Sydney stared at him with clear eyes.

"You're right, Agent Briggs. Money certainly cannot buy happiness." She gazed at her mother's lifeless body. "Obviously." She sighed a sigh heavy enough to contain the weight of the world in it, while Agent Briggs stared at her sympathetically.

"It's going to be awhile before we can piece everything together, but from what we've gathered, your mom and Harrison Daniels have been plotting this for awhile. Revenge and money are two of the most common motives that I see in my line of work and between the two of them, they had them both covered."

"I just don't understand how my mother could turn on us like that. I've never done a thing to her. It's unfathomable."

Sydney couldn't seem to tear her eyes away from her mother's body. It was macabre and morbid, but she was fascinated by the way her mother had threatened her life just minutes ago, and was now dead herself. Sydney was safe and her mother was dead. Her mind just couldn't comprehend everything...it couldn't keep up. It had been overloaded today.

"Miss Ross, I wouldn't be a bit surprised if your mother had mental issues that she kept carefully hidden from everyone. Just like Harrison Daniels. No sane person could have done what they did."

His eyes beseeched her with an unspoken message- that it wasn't her fault that her mother didn't love her. She appreciated that and she had been right. Agent Briggs was a kind person.

"We're going to need your statement regarding everything that has happened, but it can wait until tomorrow. I think it's best if you go to the hospital to be with your father today."

She nodded as he squeezed her elbow, before he left her to continue working on the scene. Stephen sidled up to take the agent's place.

"Danny's mother was beyond relieved. She's on her way over. I told her that the FBI was here and that they would more than likely want to talk to her, as well. What a nightmare, Sydney."

"Well, that's the understatement of the decade."

She turned and kissed him on the mouth, savoring the feel of his soft, warm lips as he wrapped his arms around her and held her close. She was safe in his arms. If she had ever doubted it, she knew it now. Thirty minutes ago, she wasn't sure if she'd ever even see Stephen again, let alone stand and talk to him. She soaked in his presence now, happy in an I'm-so-happy-we're-alive type of way.

"How are you holding up?" Stephen examined her face and wiped at the blood droplets that were dried onto her cheek. It was hard telling whose blood it even was.

"Oh, you know. Like any other girl who... oh, forget it. I'm a wreck. I should be crying, but I'm not. I can't and I don't know why. I feel numb, my mother is dead, I thought you were dead, my father almost died and I feel like I could sleep for a week. I just want to pull the covers over my head and hide from the world. But on the same token, I know I'm going to be scared to close my eyes. I'm afraid of what I'll see when I do."

Stephen grabbed her and pulled her close, as she buried her face into his shirt, inhaling his familiar scent.

"Sydney, listen to me. This is over. I'm not dead and you're safe now. I promise you, I will hold you every night for the rest of your life. You'll never need to be afraid again."

His voice was assured and strong and she didn't argue with him. Instead, she changed the subject.

"Is Tom okay? I haven't seen him."

"He's fine. He's awake now and chatting with the paramedics while they check him out. The man is a talker. And he seems completely unfazed by all of this. What a remarkable guy!"

Sydney nodded. She couldn't agree more.

"Will you take me to him?"

"Of course."

Stephen guided her lightly with his hand against her back, keeping her within an arm's reach at all times. Sydney felt confident that he wouldn't allow her very far out of his sight for awhile and that was perfectly fine with her.

The paramedics had Tom reclined in the living room, resting comfortably on a couch. He had an IV tube running into his arm, but other than that, appeared normal. His wrinkled face lit up in a grin when he saw her.

"Sydney! I'm happy to see you safe and sound." He reached out for her hand and she took it, enjoying the warmth of his large gnarled mitt.

"Tom, I'm so sorry that I got you involved in all of this. I am so grateful to you. I'll never be able to repay you." She squeezed his hand as he looked at her with twinkling eyes.

"Oh, yes you can. You've got connections, little girl. Maybe you could talk to your father about voting for more tax breaks for farmers." He laughed. "Oh, I'm only joking. Kind of."

Sydney laughed, delighted that she was still able to do so. After the horror of her day, it wouldn't be unheard of if she didn't find anything funny for quite a long time.

"Tom, do you need anything? Should we send someone out to your house to feed your animals or anything?"

Tom shook his head. "Nope, little girl. They're telling me that I can go home here in a bit. I can take care of everything myself. But thank you kindly, just the same." He paused for a moment, his eyes gleaming kindly. "I'm very sorry about your mother."

Sydney felt a pang in her heart and bent down to hug the wrinkled man, whispering in his ear.

"Thank you. For everything. Any time you need anything, you call me."

He nodded. "Sure will. And Sydney, that works the other way, too. Call me anytime. I get lonely sometimes, so you can even just call me to talk. I don't text, though. Never could figure out the fascination with that." He shook his head in annoyance at the thought and Sydney smiled.

"Okay, Tom. I'll call you in a couple of days to check up on you and I promise that I won't text you." She smiled at him again before making her way across the room to where Stephen was waiting for her.

"Syd, Agent Briggs just spoke with the hospital. Your dad was just admitted for surgery. He's in critical but stable condition. They think he's going to be just fine."

Relief surged through every cell in her body as she processed the information.

"Thank God," she whispered. She leaned up to kiss Stephen on the cheek. She looked down at her blood covered clothing. It was even dried into her hair in clumps.

"I'm going to take a quick shower and then how about… we go up to the hospital?"

He smiled gently down at her.

"Sydney, I would follow you to the ends of the earth. I hope you know that."

She smiled back before she walked away. She knew.

CHAPTER SIXTEEN

"Only three more hours until I get to see you again."

Stephen's deep, husky voice filled Sydney's ear and she smiled into the phone.

She was sitting in her new apartment with her long legs draped over the side of an overstuffed white chair, staring out her living room window.

Lucky for her, her father had been in total agreement that she could live off-campus in an apartment rather than living in a dorm at Notre Dame. She wasn't sure that dorm life would agree with her now. She valued her privacy too much.

After everything that had happened, she had chosen to attend Notre Dame rather than Columbia, because Indiana was so much closer to home. It was only an hour and a half drive, if she drove fast- which she always did.

"Only three hours, hmm?" She murmured into the phone. "I wish you were here right now."

"I do, too. But I'm on the toll-road now and I'll be there soon. I'm sorry that I had to go on this book tour, sweetheart. I wish you could've come with me. You should see New York!"

She smiled again at his enthusiasm and didn't bother to mention that she had seen New York numerous times. And all of the brilliance of the lights of the Big Apple didn't compare to how she felt when she was with Stephen.

"I finally got everything unpacked. And I hung all of your clothes in the spare bedroom closet. I'm sorry, but I took up all of the space in ours."

She laughed lightly, because she knew he wouldn't care. On their first night in the new apartment, they had eaten cold Chinese on an overturned moving box. Stephen had told her right then and there that he didn't care what happened in life but that he wanted to spend every moment with her.

"I also took the liberty of turning that bedroom into an office for you. I hope you don't mind. You need somewhere to write if you're going to keep me in the lifestyle that I am accustomed."

She grinned even though he couldn't see her.

He laughed huskily into the phone. "Woman, I miss you. You're too good to me!"

She was just about to jokingly agree when the doorbell rang. She glanced up in surprise. She wasn't expecting anyone.

"Stephen, someone's here. I'll have to call you back, okay? I love you."

She tossed her phone onto the couch as she crossed the room to the front door. She peeked through the peephole, only to find Christian Price standing in the hallway with flowers in his hand. Her breath froze in her throat as old emotions came rumbling back. They hadn't exactly parted on the best terms. She opened the door.

"Christian! What in the world are you doing here?"

She smiled, but her expression was puzzled.

"Shouldn't you be at Princeton right now getting ready for a big game or something?" She tried to keep her voice light, but underneath the surface, she was boiling with curiosity.

"Yes." Christian grinned the dimpled grin that used to take her breath away. "But I'm home for the weekend. And I needed to see you."

He handed her the flowers. "These are for you, of course."

"Um, thanks. But what are they for? It's not my birthday."

"Well, let's just say they're a peace offering. Can we do that?" His smile was hopeful, as he reached for her hand. "I know that I let you down. And I feel really guilty about that."

She drew her hand away.

"No offense, Chris, but you're not getting into my pants."

She smiled jokingly, which he immediately returned.

"Um, no offense, Syd- but I've been there, done that." He dodged as she slugged him on the arm. "Ow- you've gotten a pretty good right hook since the last time I saw you."

"I've been taking self-defense lessons," she replied proudly. "I could lay you out if I wanted to."

"Well, let's not get too carried away," Christian grinned.

Sydney shook her head and let it slide. It had been easy to slide back into their old joking comradery but she knew he was here for a reason.

"Chris, it's nice to see you. But why don't you come in and tell me why you are here?" She swung the door open and gestured for him to come in.

"Can I get you anything to drink?"

He settled himself into the couch as Sydney went into the kitchen to put the flowers into water. "A water would be nice- thanks!"

He looked around her cozy living room.

"Nice place, Syd," he said approvingly. "I couldn't get my parents to agree to off-campus living."

Sydney handed him a bottle of water.

"Well, my dad has been very accommodating. Since everything..." her voice trailed off.

It had been several months since everything had happened and she still didn't like to talk about it. She wasn't sure that she ever would.

"That's why I'm here." Christian spoke so low that Sydney had to strain her ears to hear him. "I'm sorry, Syd. About everything."

She glanced at his handsome face in surprise.

"You drove all the way here to apologize? You could've called. My number is still the same."

"It wouldn't have been the same. The FBI agent... what's his name? Agent Briggs? Anyway, he had to do some follow-up interviews with me and he told me that the police detective had told you that I said that the baby wasn't mine and that you were probably knocked up at a party... all kinds of things."

Sydney nodded painfully. The memories were still fresh and Christian's lies were still hurtful even though they had been overshadowed by everything else.

"Sydney, he lied. I never told him anything like that. You can ask my parents, if you don't believe me. They were there during my interview with him. I told him the truth- that you and I had been dating for months and that I loved you, but I just wasn't ready to be a dad."

He stared pensively out the window.

"Do you think you can ever forgive me for that, Syd? For not wanting to be a dad?"

Sydney's heart throbbed. At one time, she had wanted to strangle him for leaving her to face everything alone. But she could see now that he was still the same Christian, the one that she had fallen in love with. Loveable, playful Christian. And of course he hadn't been ready to have a child. With his personality, he probably wouldn't be ready until he was 40. She leaned over and squeezed his hand.

"Chris, I meant what I told you at the time. I didn't hold it against you then and I still don't. That was your decision and you had every right to make it. But I am very happy to hear that the detective was lying. It was heartbreaking at the time."

He leaned over to hug her.

"Sydney, I haven't been able to forget something you said once. You said that every girl remembers her 'first' and that you wanted me to remember you even though you weren't mine."

She nodded. She remembered that conversation clearly.

"I'll always remember you. Everything about you—the way you twirl your hair when you are relaxed, the way you laugh when you are nervous, the way you drive much too fast... we've known each other a long time. And a piece of me will always love you. I'm really, really sorry about everything that happened. You didn't deserve any of it."

He leaned over and hugged her tightly again and she let him, closing her eyes at the familiarity of his scent. He had worn the same cologne since they were in junior high. And it suited him.

"Christian, you're a really good person. I'm glad I was with you and I wish you nothing but the best." She kissed his cheek and sat back in her chair, studying him curiously.

"So, tell me. Who's the new chick? Because I know you have one."

He laughed as he allowed himself to be led into a lighter conversation

"Well, obviously she isn't you, but she's still pretty great."

And for the next fifteen minutes or so, he shared details of his life with Sydney and she listened with friendly interest.

"So, let me get this straight. You forgot to pick her up at a restaurant and she didn't even get mad? You'd better keep her." Sydney swirled her water around in the bottom of the bottle while she laughed.

Christian laughed too and glanced at his watch.

"Okay. As much as I hate to, I should probably get going. I'm supposed to have dinner with my parents." He grimaced as he stood up.

"Well, by all means, give them my love." Sydney smiled as she allowed Christian to pull her to her feet.

He wrinkled his brow. "I'm sorry about that, too, Syd. You know, about the way my mom treated you. She has a temper sometimes."

"Don't worry about it." And Sydney meant it. Christian's mom had been worried about her son's future. It was a natural reaction and she wasn't going to hold it against her.

"Don't be a stranger, Syd." Christian leaned down to kiss her cheek. "Call me anytime and come up to a Princeton football game sometime. I could use a familiar face from home in the crowd."

"Maybe I'll do that. Good-bye, Christian. Drive safely."

He looked back one time and then strode confidently down the hallway. Sydney watched his retreating back with a reminiscent smile. She had been speaking the truth. She was glad that they had been together. She had learned so much.

Digging through the couch cushions, she found the television remote and clicked the TV on. The local news channel was running yet another follow-up story on the whole Ross family scandal. It seemed that she would never be able to escape it.

The blonde reporter dressed in a dark mauve suit matter-of-factly discussed the fall-out from the scandal.

"Yes, Maureen... today, Illinois Senator Randall Ross returned to Washington after a several month hiatus. He has been in seclusion in his Highland Park mansion for months after his wife conspired with an Illinois policeman to murder her own family.

"Luckily for Senator Ross and their daughter, Sydney, their devious plan wasn't carried out although several others lost their lives in the brutal attack, including Ohio senator Paul Hayes. Senator Ross returned from his hiatus only this week and says that he is feeling much better and is looking forward to once again serving his constituents."

Sydney stared at the smiling picture of her father and sighed. She loved her father and was so happy that their relationship had taken on a healthy, new life. She was also thankful that Jillian and Harrison's lies had never seen the light of day.

But none of that changed the fact that she was probably never going to enjoy the political lifestyle. She hated living in a fishbowl. Even here, in the smallish town of South Bend, she was recognized wherever she went. The only place she had any privacy was in her apartment. It was her very own fortress of solitude.

She grabbed Stephen's book and headed for the bathroom, intent on taking a hot bubble bath. She ran the water and tied her hair up before stepping into the bubbles. The apartment sized bath-tub certainly wasn't her sunken marble tub back home, but it would work.

She didn't even realize that she had fallen asleep until Stephen's voice woke her up.

"So, do you come here often, beautiful?"

She opened her eyes to find Stephen bending down next to the bathtub, lifting the book off of her chest. It was a wonder that she hadn't dropped it into the water.

"You know, I know that author. I could probably get him to autograph it for you.

He'll be so happy to know that you're reading it for the millionth time."

His warm, chocolate eyes were crinkled at the corners as he smiled at her. Sydney leaned up to kiss him on his warm lips and wrapped her arms around his neck, enjoying the jolt of electricity that she received every single time their lips met. She was pretty sure that she would never tire of it.

A devious thought entered her mind and quickly before he could anticipate it, she pulled him down hard until he landed in the mountain of bubbles on top of her. Water sloshed out of the tub onto the floor, but she didn't even notice. She was too busy laughing in self-satisfaction.

"Now was that really necessary?" Stephen laughed as he gazed directly into her eyes, wearing his love for her like a badge.

"I think it was. I've missed you. I never, ever want you to leave me again."

"That's something you don't need to worry about, Syd. If I ever do have to leave you, it will always be brief. And I'll always come right back."

Pushing the bubbles out of his way, he pulled her to him and kissed her until she believed it. She finally broke away so that

she could breathe and sighed contentedly.
Money couldn't buy happiness, but she had
managed to find it anyway.   She closed her
eyes and smiled.

The End

To read more about Sydney and
Stephen, read book two in the American
Princess series, *Glass Castles*.

About The Author

Courtney Cole is a novelist who lives close to Lake Michigan with her family (aka domestic zoo), her pet iPad and her favorite cashmere socks.

Other works by Courtney: The Bloodstone Saga (*Every Last Kiss, Fated, With My Last Breath, My Tattered Bonds*), The Moonstone Saga (*Soul Kissed, Soul Bound*), and *Guardian*.

To learn more about Courtney, visit her website, www.courtneycolewrites.com

ACKNOWLEDGMENTS

As always, I would like to thank my family for putting up with me. Trust me, it's a full-time job. Thank you for being my biggest fans.

I also want to thank my friend and partner in crime, Fisher Amelie. Thank you for all of the authorly advice and for telling me that *Princess* was amazing. Thank you for the ranting sessions. And hand-holding. And for talking me down from 5 million ledges. And for making me laugh when I might cry otherwise.

Same goes to Michelle Leighton. Thank you for all the late night texting. And SOS emails . And brainstorming. And girl talk. And for Bo.

Craig Ellis, thank you to the world's best editor. You saw this manuscript when it was just an unpolished piece of coal. You told me it was a diamond and you've been helping me polish it ever since. Thank you.

And a gigantic thank you to Tammy Luke, my goddess of a cover artist. Thank you for saving me from multiple panic attacks. Your work is awesome and speaks for itself.

CPSIA information can be obtained at www.ICGtesting.com
Printed in the USA
LVOW10s1629010316

477310LV00020B/816/P